P9-CEV-787

"TOO SMART" JONES
and the Cat's Secret

6

A GILBERT MORRIS MYSTERY

KINGSWAY
CHRISTIAN
SCHOOL
LIBRARY

MOODY PRESS
CHICAGO

© 2000 by
GILBERT MORRIS

All rights reserved. No part of this book may be reproduced in any form without permission in writing from the publisher, except in the case of brief quotations embodied in critical articles or reviews.

ISBN: 0-8024-4030-4

1 3 5 7 9 10 8 6 4 2

Printed in the United States of America

Contents

Birthday Present

The backyard of the Jones residence was crowded with boys and girls. Juliet Jones was celebrating her birthday—and it looked as if every friend she had was helping her celebrate. She was dressed for the party. She had on a pretty light blue dress with a white sailor collar.

Suddenly somebody nudged her in the ribs.

"Oof!" Juliet grunted and spun around.

Her brother, Joe, gave her a big grin. He was wearing a colorful Hawaiian shirt, a pair of tan pants, and dingy Nike running shoes.

"Happy birthday! Looks like you made quite a haul." He motioned toward a table laden with presents. "Do you feel smarter today now that you're twelve? But, no! Too Smart Jones *couldn't* get any smarter."

Juliet grabbed a handful of Joe's hair and gave it a yank. "Don't call me Too Smart Jones!" she snapped.

Juliet had been given the nickname "Too Smart Jones" some time ago. She was doing so well in school that someone said, "You're just too smart," and the nickname had stuck. "I wish you'd forget that name, and I wish everybody else would."

"Well, maybe they'll start calling me Too Good Looking Jones." Joe grinned again. Then he looked over the guests. "Looks like everybody's here. I'm about ready for opening presents. Then we can get started with the serious business—like eating ice cream and cake."

"We're going to have the ice cream and cake *first,*" Juliet said firmly.

Joe groaned. "Boy, you have to run everything, don't you? Well, it's your birthday. But Mom sure did a good job on that cake. There. I think she's about ready to let us at it."

Mrs. Jones was coming from the house carrying a huge cake with white icing. Twelve candles brightly burned on the top. Behind her, carrying a container of ice cream, came Juliet's father. He caught Juliet's eye as they approached the table. "About time for the feast," he said.

"Everybody gather around for the candle lighting," her mother called.

"Let me light them." Joe reached for the

box of matches his father had taken from his pocket. He carefully lit the twelve candles, then blew out the match. "There you go," he said to Juliet. "Make a wish."

"Make it a good one," Chili Williams said. He was a strongly built boy with large ears. He liked chili so much that Chili had become his nickname. "I hope your wish comes true."

Juliet, who liked Chili very much, flashed a grin at him. Then she made a fun wish and blew out the candles with one big breath.

"I always said you were windy." Flash Gordon was in his wheelchair because a car accident had crippled him. He had reddish hair and cheerful green eyes that seemed to glow. He looked up at Juliet's mother. "Didn't you make cake for anybody else, Mrs. Jones? I can eat that much myself."

As a laugh went up, Juliet said, "You can have the first piece, Flash." She removed the smoking candles and cut an enormous wedge. Then she placed it on a blue plastic plate. Adding a fork, she gave it to Flash.

He immediately took a huge bite. "Ooh, that's good!" he said. "I couldn't have done better myself."

Juliet cut cake for everyone. Her father added a huge dollop of ice cream beside every piece. Her mother poured pink punch. Soon the only sound was of boys and girls murmuring and giggling as they ate.

Juliet sat between Samuel and Delores Del Rio, ages eleven and nine. Both of them had black hair and dark eyes and were very nice looking. Delores was a special friend.

"Well," Sam said, "you're getting to be an old woman." He leaned forward and studied her face. "Yep. I can see those wrinkles right now."

Delores picked up a strand of Juliet's hair. "Yes, and here's a gray hair."

"You're over the hill. No doubt about that." Sam nodded solemnly. "I'd better get you a cane."

"Yeah, and you can start dyeing your hair, too—getting all that gray out of it," Joe added.

Flash rolled his wheelchair around. "Yep, old lady Jones is over the hill."

"You all can stop picking on me," Juliet said, but she really didn't mind.

"No, we shouldn't pick on our elders." Joe winked at the others. "Let's remember this lady's age and be polite to her."

Juliet enjoyed their teasing. As a matter of fact, she enjoyed her friends. They were all being homeschooled by their parents or grandparents. And they were all members of the Oakwood Support Group for homeschoolers. In spite of missing out on some things in public school, Juliet was very happy with the education she was getting.

After the boys and girls had filled up on cake, punch, and ice cream, Joe took over.

"Now it's time for games! The first thing we do is pin the tail on the donkey. Hey, Billy," he joked. "I guess you're ugly enough to be the donkey."

The boys and girls laughed, and Billy Rollins scowled.

"I'm better looking then you are! I heard when you were a baby you were so ugly your mama had to tie a pork chop around your neck to get the dog to play with you."

A laugh went up again, and this time Billy Rollins grinned. He actually was not very nice a great deal of the time. However, he seemed to be mostly on his good behavior today and soon joined in the games.

Mr. and Mrs. Jones sat over to one side watching the games. Finally Juliet's dad got to his feet and said, "Hey, kids! How about calling the Olympics off for a while and let's have the birthday girl open her presents."

"All right!" Joe cried. He grabbed Juliet by one hand, and Chili Williams grabbed her by the other. Together they pulled her over to the gift table. "There," Joe said. "Let's see what you've got in all this loot."

Juliet felt a little embarrassed to have everybody watching her. But she picked up one present and looked at it. "What pretty wrapping paper!"

"That's from me," Billy Rollins said. "I didn't wrap it myself, but I picked it out."

Juliet opened the package and saw that it was a book that she had wanted for a long time. "Why, Billy, what a nice surprise!"

"Surprise!" he snorted. "You've told everybody you know for the past six months that you wanted that book! If I ever heard hinting for a present, that was it."

Juliet thought that wasn't very polite, but everybody laughed. She picked up another package.

"That's from both of us," Delores Del Rio said. "We had to pool our money to get it, but I hope you like it."

Carefully Juliet peeled back the red and white paper and found a small box. She lifted the lid and gasped. "Oh, it's a charm bracelet! How beautiful!"

"Well—" Sam grinned "—you couldn't pass by the jewelry store window without stopping to stare at it. I think you made it pretty plain that's what you wanted. That's what I like about you, Juliet. It's easy to find out what you want because you always come right out and say it."

"Oh, I do not!" Juliet said. She opened another present then, the one from her closest friend, Jenny White.

"I hope you like it," Jenny said shyly.

Opening the package, Juliet saw that it was a very large jigsaw puzzle. She looked at the picture on the front. It was an ocean scene with all sorts of different colored tropical fish—red, green, blue, orange. "Oh, this will be so much fun, Jenny!" she said. "Now we won't have to worry about what to do on a rainy afternoon. We'll put it right on a card table in the living room, and you can come over and we can work on it."

"That'll be fun," Jenny said. "I'm glad you like it."

At last Juliet had opened all the presents, and she was pleased with all of them. She was, however, surprised that there was nothing in the pile of presents from her father or mother —and nothing from Joe, either. She tried to keep her disappointment from showing, though. She said, "Well, thank you all very much. I love all of my presents. I couldn't have had a nicer birthday party!"

At that moment Juliet's mother came out of the house carrying a wicker basket. It was covered with bright red cloth, tied at the handle of the basket with a yellow bow. "There's one more present," she said. "Did you think we hadn't gotten you anything?"

Juliet blushed a little because that was exactly what had popped into her mind. She started to speak, but then she heard something move inside the basket. Her eyes flew to her parents' faces, and she saw they were both grinning widely. She grabbed for the basket and opened the top. And then she let out a squeal. "Oh, how darling!" she cried.

Carefully she reached inside and lifted out a beautiful kitten, a black one with white mittens. She felt as though her face would break in two, she was grinning so broadly. "What a darling kitten!" she said, and she hugged it against her, smelling the clean, sweet smelling fur.

The Joneses' dog had died a few months earlier. Juliet had loved Boris, and she had begged for another pet. But her parents said that they weren't quite sure that she was old enough to really take care of a pet. And they had warned her that if she ever did get a dog or a cat, it would be her responsibility. Juliet had just about given up.

But now she put her cheek alongside the tiny kitten and felt wonderfully happy.

"Mrow!"

"You're hugging that kitten too hard!" her father said. "Don't squeeze all the breath out of it!"

"Oh, I'm sorry, kitten!"

Her friends crowded around, and each had to stroke it. The kitten was looking about with wide eyes.

"It doesn't seem to be afraid at all."

"No. He's very outgoing," her mother said. "I got him from a litter of a friend of mine, and he was the finest one of the lot. He was the alpha cat."

"What's an *alpha* cat?" Juliet asked.

"In most litters, one animal will be stronger and smarter than the rest. It's called the alpha cat. And this one was the alpha cat."

"Oh, no! Too Smart Jones got a too smart cat!" Billy Rollins howled.

Juliet thought she had never been so excited. She had longed for a kitten for so long, and now here he was.

"I'm going to call him Boots," she said. "The white on his feet looks exactly like little white boots."

While all the youngsters were still crowded around, a loud voice said, "Hey, let me get through here, will you!"

Juliet looked up to see Joe coming. He had a large box in his hands. It also was brightly wrapped, and he was grinning from ear to ear. "You think I'd forgotten your birthday?"

"Well, it wouldn't be the first time you forgot something." But Juliet grinned back.

"Here. Check this out," he said and set the box down.

Juliet untied the ribbon, ripped off the paper, and opened the top. "Oh, it's a litter box!"

"Yeah, and a month's supply of cat litter!"

"And look at this!" Juliet cried. She held up a pink rubber mouse. It made a squeaking sound. "It's a cat's toy. And he heard it, didn't you, Boots?"

The kitten indeed had heard the squeaking.

When Juliet put both kitten and mouse on the ground, he pounced on it.

"That's a fierce cat you got there, Too Smart," Flash Gordon said. "He's going to be a winner."

For a while everybody watched Boots play with the ribbon and the wrapping paper. He seemed to like the attention. Then everyone had to touch him again and hold him at least once. When Juliet got him back, he went to sleep in her arms. And then the party was over.

After all her friends were gone, Juliet helped clean up. Then she watched Boots as he slept. When he woke up, she played with him. And when she went to bed that night, he slept beside her on her pillow.

"You're so beautiful," she breathed, stroking his soft, silky fur. She went to sleep and had wonderful dreams of the days to come with her new pet.

A New Friend

"Aw, who wants to go to an old nursing home!" Joe grumbled. He glanced at Juliet, who told him to hush.

The homeschool support group was meeting for their monthly get together. Mrs. Arthur Boyd, who liked to run things, was announcing their new project.

"Children," she said, "we're going to visit a nursing home." She was a rather bossy lady, Juliet thought. She was very proud of her twins, Helen and Ray. Now she frowned at the groan that went up.

"Who wants to go to an old nursing home?" Billy Rollins complained. "I want to do something else."

"Yeah, let's do something more fun than that!" Ray said, scowling at his mother.

"Now, this will be a wonderful thing for you all to do," she said.

"Why, Mom, we don't even visit our *own* grandparents," Helen Boyd said. "Why can't we go to Disney World or someplace interesting?"

"Now, children, I don't want to hear any more about this!" Mrs. Boyd said. "It's been decided by all of the parents. We do fun things, but this can be fun too. You can meet some very interesting people in a nursing home. It'll make you more aware of the older generation."

"I'm already aware of the older generation," Billy Rollins complained. "They're always making me do things I don't want to do."

"Aw, be quiet, Billy!" But Flash Gordon grinned. He leaned over from his wheelchair and rapped Billy sharply on the head. "You'd complain if they hung you with a piece of new rope!"

"Yeah!" Chili said. "It'll be fun. I been to a nursing home. My grandma was in one until she died. I went to see her a lot."

"But that's your *kinfolks,*" Billy said. He was always grumbling about something. Now he pouted and sat back with a stubborn look on his face.

"It would be a *good* thing to do," Juliet said. "I'll bet those old people get lonesome there."

"That's the spirit," Mrs. Boyd said. "Now, I've made plans. We'll leave from here at one o'clock tomorrow."

The next day was mild, though the sun was hiding behind the clouds. There was the fresh smell of spring in the air. Mrs. Boyd and two other parents accompanied the boys and girls as they made their way down Washington Avenue.

There was the usual fooling around along the way. Billy Rollins and Samuel Del Rio had to be quieted down, and Flash Gordon felt he just had to cut some wheelies in his wheelchair. It was always amazing to Juliet that he could roll that chair with his arms faster than most of them could run.

"Hey, wait up, Flash," Sam called out. "The rest of us don't have wheels!"

"You'll just have to run faster," Flash yelled. "Don't be such slowpokes!"

Then they reached the Oakwood Nursing Home. It was a light brown brick building, next door to the park. When they went inside, Juliet saw that the walls were freshly painted. The place even smelled of new paint. The floors were polished to a high gloss.

Mrs. Boyd was greeted by the social worker in charge.

"Oh, you've brought the boys and girls!" she said. She was a kind-looking woman with blonde hair. "Some of our people get so lonely.

Just to talk to anybody is a treat for them." She looked over the group and said, "Thank you for coming, children. I appreciate it so much."

"You'll have to give us some advice. Most of them have never been to a nursing home before," Mrs. Boyd said.

"And of course I will. We have a nice sitting room out here where the people gather. Come this way."

Juliet whispered to Jenny, "I'm a little bit scared. I like the idea, but I don't know how to talk to old people."

"Don't be silly," Jenny said. "You talk to Mr. and Mrs. Del Rio all the time." Ramon and Maria Del Rio were the grandparents of Samuel and Delores.

"But that's not the same thing. They're well and healthy and live at home. Some of these people are very old and can't even take care of themselves."

"It'll be all right," Jenny said. "Remember what we learned in Sunday school last Sunday. About trusting in the Lord with all your heart. Don't lean on your own understanding."

Juliet flashed her a grateful look. "You always have a Bible verse for everything," she said with admiration.

They trooped down a long hall and came out into a large room where many older people were sitting. One side was completely covered with windows. Juliet could see large trees and flowerbeds and squirrels playing. A man was cutting grass, and another was working in the flowerbeds.

"Now," the lady in charge said, "you may just go up and talk to any of the people here about anything you want to. Tell them your name. Most of them will be very glad to talk to you. If some of them aren't, just go to someone else."

At once Billy Rollins went up to an old man who was playing cards by himself. Billy said, "Hi!"

The man looked up and blinked with surprise. "Hello," he said. "What's your name?"

"Billy Rollins. What are you playing?"

"Solitaire."

"Do you know how to play 'Go Fish'?"

The man smiled at him. He had silvery hair and mild blue eyes. "I used to when I was about your age. I'll bet I can beat you."

"Bet you can't." Billy Rollins sat down, and the two started a game.

Across the room, Jack Tanner, a tall thin boy of ten, saw a man watching them. "Hi," he said. "My name's Jack Tanner."

"My name's Ed Matthews."

"You like to fish, Mr. Matthews?"

"Can't fish now, but I used to before I came here. I guess I liked fishing better than anything else."

Soon they were talking about fishing. The man seemed happy, and Jack seemed happy.

Jenny White chose a woman who was very small and delicate. At first the woman did not speak. But Jenny kept talking. Before long she found out that the woman had been a dancer in the *Nutcracker* when she was young.

Finding someone was easy for Flash Gordon because he always liked to talk. He spotted a man in a wheelchair. The man was wearing a Texas Rangers ball cap. "Hi," he said. "I'm Flash Gordon. You like the Rangers?"

"Never missed a game before I came here. I lived in Dallas. You like baseball?" He was very old indeed. Even his voice was feeble.

"I do. I'm gonna play someday."

"What are you doing in that wheelchair?" the man asked.

"I had an accident, but I think the Lord's going to heal me."

"Well, that'll be good. Then you can play baseball."

Juliet felt a little shy. But she finally saw a lady sitting by herself over in a corner. She was half sheltered by a huge artificial tree, and she was watching what was going on without smiling.

Juliet took a deep breath and said to herself, *Well, I've got to start. Everybody else has found someone to talk to.* She came to a stop in front of the woman by the tree. The woman, like everyone else here, had gray hair. She was wearing a string of pearls around her neck and had on a bright purple dress. "Hello," Juliet said. "My name is Juliet Jones."

The woman looked up at her, smiling. "My name is Jones, too. Eliza Jones."

"Oh, isn't that something! Maybe we're related."

"I doubt that," Eliza Jones said. "There are so many of us Joneses in the world."

"But maybe we are," Juliet said. She pulled up a chair. "I always think that things don't just happen, but the Lord makes them happen."

"Well, maybe so. Who are all you young people anyway? What are you doing here?"

Juliet quickly explained, and Eliza Jones took a deep breath. "Well, that's so nice of you to come."

"How long have you been here? Tell me about yourself."

Words came rushing out of Mrs. Eliza Jones, then. It was like water rushing out of an opened dam. She told Juliet about her childhood, about her family, and about the pets she used to have. It seemed she could go on forever about her cats.

"Oh, do you like cats? Me too."

"Yes, I've had many cats. I miss them all terribly. Come with me, Juliet. I want to show you something."

Mrs. Jones seemed healthier than some of the old people. She even walked without the help of a cane. She led Juliet down the corridor and then turned into a very attractive room. She said, "Look at this."

Juliet saw that the walls were covered with pictures. She exclaimed, "Why, these are all pictures of cats and dogs!"

"Yes. All my pets. Oh, I loved every one of them so much. You see this dog? His name was Hector. He liked to sit on my feet. Followed me around. No matter where I stopped, he would plop right down on my feet." Old Mrs. Jones looked rather pretty as she laughed.

"I've got a new pet," Juliet told her. "A new kitten named Boots. He has white feet."

"What color is he?"

"All black except for his feet."

"I always liked black cats."

"Did you have some?"

"Oh my, yes! Over the years I must have had half a dozen. I've got pictures of all of them."

"You must love animals."

"Yes, I do. Almost all kinds."

Mrs. Jones listened to Juliet tell about Boots. She said, "I wish you'd bring him to see me sometime."

"Maybe I can. I'll ask. He'd love to come and visit you."

"Would you really do that?"

"Sure I would!"

"That would be wonderful! I get lonesome for animals."

Mrs. Jones had albums full of pictures of her pets. They sat in her room while Juliet looked at all the photographs.

"My family—they're busy. They can only get here about twice a month to visit me," Mrs. Jones said. "I get very lonely at times. I miss them just like I do my pets."

Juliet felt very sorry for Mrs. Eliza Jones. "I'll be sure to bring Boots to see you," she promised.

The time at the nursing home passed quickly. When they were all outside again, Juliet said, "That was a good idea you had, Mrs. Boyd, coming to the nursing home. It was actually fun!"

Billy Rollins said, "I say let's have a ball game. That's what's really fun."

Billy always had to be troublesome. They had not gone far before he gave one of the smaller children a shove.

"Don't do that!" Juliet said and quickly helped the girl up.

"She's just clumsy." He pushed Juliet then. "And all I've heard out of you is about that old Mrs. Jones and how interesting she is!"

"Well, she *is* interesting, and she's smart too."

"Oh no. Too Smart Jones has found a 'Too Smart' friend!" Billy said loudly. "Well, my new friend is better than yours. He's going to teach me to play all kinds of cards."

Billy continued to pester Juliet until finally Joe put himself between them. He said, "Billy, keep your hands to yourself!"

Billy said, "Aw, who do you think you are?" But he walked off.

"Thanks, Joe," Juliet said. "Billy sometimes can be nice, but then he can be a real pest."

Joe winked at her. "Both of us are kind of like that, too, don't you think?"

Juliet did not forget her promise. The very next day she took Boots to see Mrs. Eliza Jones. The old lady loved the kitten, and he seemed to like her. She played with him, using a piece of ribbon. She laughed when he slapped at it and got it wound around his feet. She found a saucer and poured a little milk for him. She chuckled when he got it all over his face.

"Oh, what an affectionate kitten!" she said when he licked her nose.

"He seems to love just everybody," Juliet said.

The visit was very good, but then Juliet had to take Boots and go home. She saw that was hard on Mrs. Jones.

"I wish you didn't have to go," the old lady said sadly.

"I do too, but I'll come back. I promise."

Juliet kept that promise too. She went by the nursing home at least twice a week and sometimes three times. She saw that old Mrs. Jones, who had loved her own pets so much, was falling in love with Boots.

One Thursday when Juliet was ready to leave, Mrs. Jones hugged Boots. She kissed the sleepy kitten between his ears and said, "You're such a precious kitten. I love you so much."

Juliet hated to take Boots away from her, but it was time to go. "Boots, say good-bye to Mrs. Jones."

Boots yawned, stretched, and then cuddled himself up against Juliet.

"I'll see you again soon."

"Thank you for bringing him. Not many girls would be as thoughtful as you've been, Juliet," Mrs. Jones said sadly.

Juliet started for home, thinking, *I'm glad I can do this. It makes me feel like I'm helping someone. I think it must be the kind of thing that pleases the Lord, too.* All the way home, she held Boots tightly. She told him, "You're the best birthday present anyone ever got, Boots."

The Missing Cat

"I sure get tired of thinking about the weather."

Juliet looked across the room to where Joe was sitting at his desk. It was the middle of the afternoon, but they were catching up on some schoolwork. Their father had made them a special schoolroom, where they kept their books and papers and supplies. The walls were covered with maps and pictures of famous buildings. Models of airplanes hung from the ceiling, for one of Joe's projects had to do with aircraft.

At the moment, he looked disgusted. "I don't see why we have to know so much about the weather. I think this new project is dumb!"

"Dad doesn't think so," Juliet said calmly. She was at her own desk, making an enlargement of a drawing. It was great fun. This particular picture was a drawing of the Empire

State Building in New York. It had been only about two inches high, but she had learned how to change it into a bigger size on large drawing paper. She carefully worked on the spire for a few moments before she said, "Joe, you always complain about whatever project we have."

"I do not!" he said indignantly. "When I was making the model windmill, I didn't complain about that, did I?"

"No, you don't complain about anything you can make with your hands," Juliet admitted. "But we've got to do things we don't want to do sometimes. Things that use just our minds. That's the way education is."

"Well, I just want to do what I want to do."

"All of us would *like* to do just what we want to do, but we really can't."

"Why not?"

"Because nothing would ever get done."

"Some of the stuff we do doesn't *need* to get done!"

"Now you're just being silly!"

"Some of the stuff we do is silly."

"Just go to work, Joe!"

He looked down, muttering about weather and different kinds of clouds and evaporation as he studied.

Suddenly Boots leaped from his place on a bookcase onto Joe's desk. Boots liked to climb anything. As soon as he grew big enough, Juliet thought, he would probably wind up on top of the house.

Obviously glad for an interruption, Joe picked up a ruler and held it out. Boots slapped at it with his paw. He crouched down with his rear in the air and switched his tail. Then he made a leap and pinned the ruler down. Joe giggled.

Juliet watched what was happening. "You'd better quit playing with Boots and do your work."

"I can play with him and work at the same time."

"No, you can't."

"Yes, I can!"

"You'd better let me take him." Juliet crossed the room and picked up Boots. She was wearing a lime green sweater, her favorite color, and he sunk his claws into it. When she sat down, she tried to pry him loose. The kitten's claws were caught, though, and she had to work very carefully. Then she put him in her lap and dangled a bit of yarn. He leaped into the air, trying to catch it.

"Now *you're* playing with him! What's the difference? Why can you play with him, and I can't?"

"Well, I'm about through with my work."

"So am I," Joe said quickly. "Anyway, all I've got to do is learn how to identify clouds."

"I know what to do," Juliet said. "Let's go

outside. It's a nice day, and we'll see how many clouds we can identify."

Five minutes later, Juliet and Joe were out behind the house. They were lying flat on their backs, staring up at the sky.

"Look there, Joe. That cloud looks like a bunny."

"It looks like a bear."

"I think it looks like a bunny. Don't you, Boots?"

Boots had been kneading his tiny claws into Juliet's stomach. She picked him up and turned his head to face the sky. He squirmed, and she laughed and put him down. "Doesn't look like anything to you, does it?"

"Look over there," Joe said. "See that cloud? It looks like a train engine. And that one, it looks like an arrowhead."

Juliet said, "Never mind what they look like. What kind of cloud is that one right there?"

"That's a cirrus cloud."

"Well, that's right," Juliet said. "You have learned something. What about that one?"

"Altostratus. And that one over there is cumulus," he said triumphantly. "Now, will you let me alone about clouds?"

Juliet was always impressed with how much Joe knew. He could do almost any kind of project, but he had to like it and be interested in it. If he didn't, or wasn't, he got bored and loafed.

"I wish you liked math, Joe."

"Why?"

"Because you can do stuff you like real good."

"Yeah, I guess so. I just can't make myself concentrate when I'm bored. It's too hard."

For a while they lay daydreaming and looking for different sorts of figures in the clouds. Boots began jumping at a large green bug that was flying about. He would spring into the air and almost turn a somersault. But he always landed back on his feet.

"Look at that. He's like an acrobat. If I could turn flips like that and land on my feet, I could get a job with the circus," Joe said.

"Cats are real acrobatic. Look at what he's doing now. He's chasing that butterfly."

Boots made wild leaps after the yellow-and-black butterfly. His tiny claws slashed the air. But he never caught it, and he finally fell backward into a puddle. He came out shaking his paws one at a time, which made both Joe and Juliet laugh.

"He doesn't like baths," Joe said. "I don't like them myself too much. Think of all the soap and water we'd save if we quit taking baths."

"And think of how we'd smell!"

"If everybody smelled bad, nobody would notice anybody else."

"Oh, don't be silly! I read somewhere that

tigers are good swimmers. I bet Boots could swim."

"Well, let's put him in the fish pond and see."

Joe started to get up, but Juliet jerked him back. "You leave him alone! I'd better not catch you putting him in the fish pond!"

They lay looking at the sky again until Juliet grew sleepy. Boots ran and jumped and played. He came back from time to time and jumped on her stomach.

Finally Joe got up, groaning. He said, "I guess I'd better go finish my work."

"I'll be up in a minute." Juliet sat up and took Boots into her lap. Then she forgot the cat and thought for a while about the book she had been reading. When she decided to go inside, she noticed for the first time that Boots was gone.

"Boots?"

She did not see him anywhere.

"Come, Boots. Where are you?"

But no kitten came.

Juliet got to her feet and looked around. She began walking about the backyard, which was thickly planted with azaleas and other flowers. *He could be hiding in any of them,* she thought.

"Boots, don't you hide from me!" Juliet cried. And then she began to get a little nervous. "Here, kitty, kitty, kitty!" She searched all over the backyard. Now she was really concerned. *He must have gotten away. But where can he be?*

At that moment she looked across the yard and caught just a glimpse of black and white.

"Boots, you come back here! Don't you go into that hedge!"

But the kitten paid no attention. He disappeared into the bushes.

Juliet ran to the hedge. She tried to push through. But it was the thick old hedge that separated the Jones property from their neighbors. There was no way for her to get through it.

She began yelling loudly, "Boots, you come back here!" But she knew that was a useless thing to do.

At that moment the back door opened, and she heard her mother's voice. "What are you yelling about, Juliet?"

"It's Boots. He's run away through the hedge."

"Well, get Joe, and the two of you go find him."

"Joe!" she screamed.

An upstairs window opened, and Joe stuck his red head out. "What do you want?" he demanded.

"Come and help me find Boots. He's gone through the hedge."

"All right. I'll be right down."

Joe disappeared, then reappeared at the back door. He leaped off the porch, saying, "He can't be far."

They went around the end of the hedge. Both began calling for the kitten. Sometimes they called, "Boots," and sometimes just, "Kitty, kitty, kitty." But nothing happened.

"He can't be too far!" Joe said again. "Let's go around to the back of the Williams property."

This was an empty lot. It was almost a full acre, and it belonged to people who were planning to build there someday. Right now it was nothing but pine trees and underbrush. Juliet scratched her legs on the briars as she fought her way through.

"Kitty, kitty, kitty!" she called. She stopped to look around. There was no sign of Boots.

They searched for a long time, but finally Joe said, "We might as well go home. It's almost time for supper."

"We *can't* go home! We've got to find him!"

"I think we'll have to get Mom to help—and Dad when he gets home."

Juliet hated to give up, but she knew this made sense. They turned around and went back home. Juliet was crying when she went through the door.

Her mother took one look at her and said, "You didn't find him?"

"No, Mom. We can't find him anywhere. We need all of us to go look."

Mrs. Jones acted as if she knew exactly how much Juliet loved this kitten. "All right," she said. "I'll go with you right now. I think I'd better put on jeans, though. And you too, Juliet. Look how your legs are scratched."

"I'll put on some jeans, too. But let's hurry."

Joe suddenly reached over and patted Juliet's shoulder. He almost never did that. "It'll be all right, sis. Don't worry," he said.

When their father came home an hour later, Juliet met him as he came in. He looked at her puffy red face and asked at once, "What's wrong, Juliet?"

"It's Boots. He's run away, and we can't find him."

"Well, cats roam sometimes. Let me go look."

"But, Daddy, we've all been looking already, and we can't find him!"

Mr. Jones said, "Let me go look anyhow."

Everybody went with him. But they did not find Boots.

The family went out again after supper. This time they took flashlights. They looked until almost nine o'clock. Once in a while they would check back at the house. Always Juliet hoped to find Boots at the door, scratching to get in. But all their searching proved useless.

Finally her mother said, "It's nearly bed-time, Juliet—too late to look any more tonight.

Boots will probably be on the porch when we get up in the morning."

"But—all right, Mom."

Before going to bed, Juliet called Jenny and told her what had happened.

"And, Jenny, he's gone, and we can't find him."

"Well, cats can take care of themselves," Jenny's voice came over the phone. "I'll come over and help you look first thing in the morning. But he'll probably be there when you wake up—like your mom says."

"Do you really think so?"

"Sure!"

"Well, I hope you're right."

"I am—just wait and see!"

Juliet said, "Thank you, Jenny. Come as early as you can."

Before turning out the light, Juliet knelt beside her bed and prayed, as she always did. This time she prayed for God to bring Boots home. Then she got into bed, turning so that she could see out the window. The moon was full. She hoped that Boots had found a good, safe place to spend the night.

"I wish cats weren't so much trouble," she said aloud. "I love them, but they're always getting into something."

The Return of Boots

Juliet woke up suddenly. Her eyes flew open, and she stared at the ceiling for a moment. Then she remembered. *Boots is lost!* She jumped out of bed, put on her slippers, and grabbed her robe.

Belting the robe as she ran, Juliet flew down the stairs to the back door and opened it. And there she saw what she had been hoping for—a ball of black fur curled up with its nose completely hidden.

"Boots!" She picked him up and hugged him—not too hard—and she felt like crying again. "Thank you, Lord," she said, "for answering my prayer. Boots came home."

Boots did not appear to be excited. He yawned, showing his small, needle-sharp teeth. Then he said, *"Mrow!"*

Juliet laughed. "You rascal, you! Do you know you scared me half to death!"

Boots yawned again. He looked at her with that Cheshire-cat kind of grin that Juliet had seen in the *Alice in Wonderland* video.

Then she held him closer. She sniffed and said, "What's that funny smell?"

Boots said, *"Mrow!"* and squirmed to get down.

"You smell like *perfume!* What have you been into?"

"Mrow!" he said, still squirming to get away.

"Well, let's go in the house. You must be hungry."

Juliet took a carton of milk from the refrigerator and poured some milk into a saucer. She set it on the floor.

Boots walked over and looked at the milk. Then he looked up at Juliet and yawned again. He said, *"Mrow!"* and walked away with his nose and tail in the air.

"I can't believe you're turning down milk! You always drink milk!" she said with amazement. "What have you been eating out there?"

Juliet watched as Boots walked around the kitchen, just looking at things the way that cats do. Then he jumped up onto the windowsill where the morning sun was shining in. He stretched as far as possible, flexing his claws, and then he went to sleep. Juliet could hear his purring. It was like a tiny engine inside of him.

"Well, you're some kitten," she said crossly. "I worry myself to death over you, and you don't seem to care a bit."

At that moment Juliet's mother came in. "Well, there he is!" she said with a smile. "I told you he'd probably come back."

"He was right outside the screen door, Mom. I'm so glad he's back."

"So am I. Does he seem to be all right?"

"He looks fine. He won't eat, though. He acts like he's already full."

"I don't know what he could have found to eat out there. A mouse maybe—but he's young for that."

"And he smells funny. Smell him, Mom. Where's he been?"

Mrs. Jones leaned over and sniffed at the black fur.

Juliet's mother straightened up and frowned. "He does smell a little like perfume. Probably some flowers he ran into or some kind of herb. No telling where he's been. He does seem to be all right, though."

Juliet said, "I'm going to be sure he doesn't run away again."

"Well, right now you'd better eat breakfast."

"I'm just going to eat cereal."

"We're out of cornflakes. You'll have to eat something else."

"We had a whole box yesterday morning!"

Mrs. Jones smiled. "Joe got hungry. He ate them all. You'll have to eat raisin bran."

"Oh, all right! But I don't why he has to eat all the cornflakes. He knows I like them best."

She took a box of cereal out of the cupboard and then a large white bowl. She filled it full of raisin bran, poured on milk, sugared it, and then sat down.

Her father came in and took one look at the windowsill. "I see the wanderer has come back again."

"Yes, and he seems to be all right, Daddy."

"Well, cats like to wander. Some of them anyhow. That's normal."

"Sit down, dear. Breakfast is almost ready."

Joe came in shortly after that. Then all of them kept an eye on Boots. But he did not move a whisker.

"He looks like a stuffed cat. Are you sure he's real?" Joe grinned. "How are you gonna keep him from getting lost?"

"I'm not going to let him out of my sight!"

After breakfast, Mr. Jones left for his job out at the new bridge that he was building. Joe and Juliet spent most of the morning working on their projects. Then, after lunch, Joe said, "Mom, how about if we go out and play for a while?"

"That would be fine. You both have done such a good job working this morning. I'm proud of you."

"Yeah! Come on, Juliet. Let's put on our grubbies and go out and get dirty!"

"I'll put on my new blue jeans, and I'm not going to get dirty."

They quickly changed clothes.

"Hurry up!" Joe said, as they started out the door.

But Juliet picked up the cat's carrying basket and put Boots inside it. "Just a minute. I'm taking Boots everywhere I go." The carrier had a wooden top that could be closed and latched so that Boots couldn't get out. Then she went out to her bike and fastened the basket to the bicycle's luggage rack.

"Let's go see Jenny."

"Oh, I don't want to play with a couple of girls! I'm going on to the ballpark."

"Well, I'm going to see Jenny. You do what you please."

Joe did what he pleased and rode away quickly.

Juliet pedaled over to Jenny's house. It was only four blocks away. She put down the kickstand, untied the basket, and carried it up to the front door.

It opened as soon she rang the bell, and Jenny stood there smiling. "Oh, goody! I bet you brought Boots over."

"I sure did. I'm not letting him go off again."

"How did you find him?" Jenny asked. She stepped back to let Juliet in.

"I didn't. He was just at the back door this morning when I opened it. But I don't want that to happen again."

"Come on up to the playroom." Jenny led the way upstairs, and soon the girls were busy. For a while they played with Boots and a ball of yarn. All the time they were talking about school. Both were learning how to use computers and how to use terms such as "surfing the net."

"How's Jack doing with his reading?"

Jenny's mother had married Mr. Tanner, Jack's dad. Now Jack Tanner had a mother, and Mr. Tanner was a good father to Jenny.

"Oh, he's doing better. It's helped him just to have a mom."

"How is that?"

"Oh, I don't know. It just seemed like he missed his own mother. And my mom is real good to him."

"And how are you getting along with your new dad?"

"Just fine!" Jenny beamed. "He really likes me. I missed my own dad so much. It's good to have one again."

"I see Jack's started to hang around with Billy Rollins."

"Yes, and I wish he wouldn't. I think Billy's a bad influence on him."

"And I think you're right."

"You know Billy doesn't like you because you're smart and don't have to study much."

"Don't have to study much! That's not so. I study all the time!"

"Well, you don't have to study as much as some of us do. And you *are* smart, Juliet."

Juliet said, "I'd rather be able to play the piano and sing like you can than be smart."

And then Juliet suddenly remembered that she had not been to see Mrs. Eliza Jones for a while. "Let's go to the nursing home. It always does me good to go. And I feel like it's helping Mrs. Jones and the other old people."

"Sure, I'll go with you! I met a lady there that was real nice. I've forgotten her name, though."

"She'll tell you again. Those folks are always so glad to see anybody come."

Soon they were on their bikes, pedaling down the street with Boots tied to the back of Juliet's bicycle.

"There's Sam and Delores."

"Yeah, and Flash and Chili," Jenny said. "Let's stop and see where they're going." They rolled their bikes to a stop. Jenny said, "Where are you guys going?"

Flash Gordon said, "We're going out to the ballpark and play soccer. Come on and go with us."

"We've got to go to the nursing home. I promised old Mrs. Jones I'd go see her."

"Well, when you get through, come over to the park. We'll be there for a couple of hours."

"All right," Juliet said. "You'll probably find Joe and Billy when you get there."

Flash jerked his wheels around so that the wheelchair spun in a circle. He was so good at that. He laughed and said, "Let's go! I feel like a winner today!"

Juliet watched Flash lead the group down the street. "He never gets discouraged."

"No," Jenny said thoughtfully, "he doesn't. And he keeps saying that God is going to heal him and get him out of that wheelchair someday. Do you believe that?"

"Well, God helped me get Boots back. He brought him home this morning." Then she said, "I'd give anything to see Flash able to run and play like the rest of us."

"So would I. I pray every day for him to get better."

"Do you? I do, too!" Juliet smiled. "And if that's what God wants for Flash, God will do it. Well, let's go. Mrs. Jones is always anxious to see Boots. I think she enjoys his visits more than she does mine."

As the girls got ready to pedal, Juliet heard Boots scratching at the inside of his basket. She opened the lid and peeked inside. "You just behave yourself, Boots!"

"Will he get enough air in that box?"

"Sure!"

"Well, he sure does like to travel."

"Boots is a traveling cat." Juliet smiled again. "He loves to wander!"

Ben and Lexy

At the nursing home, Juliet and Jenny went down the hall directly to Mrs. Eliza Jones's room. When Juliet looked inside, she saw that, for a change, Mrs. Jones already had visitors.

"Why, come in, Juliet." Mrs. Jones was sitting in her chair, beaming. She motioned with her hand and said, "Let me have that precious kitty."

Juliet took Boots from his basket and placed him on Mrs. Jones's lap. He began purring at once and kneading her with his claws. He always did that when he was pleased.

"Oh, I'm glad you came! I wanted you to meet my daughter-in-law and my two grandchildren. This is Ben, and this is Lexy. And this is another Mrs. Jones."

Ben was a sturdy boy about Juliet's age, and Lexy was a tiny girl with bright red hair. She was probably two years younger.

"Oh, I love kitties!" Lexy said, going at once to her grandmother's side. She began to stroke Boots, who slapped at her hand playfully.

Mrs. Eliza Jones introduced Juliet and Jenny, then said, "Sit down, girls. Stay awhile."

For some time the girls sat listening as the two women talked. Then little Lexy came over and sat down beside them. "Where did you get your pretty cat?" she asked. "I've wanted a kitten for a long time. But I don't have one yet."

"I got him for my birthday."

"My birthday's next month," Lexy said. "Maybe I'll get a kitten, too." After a while she asked, "What does Boots do all day besides play?"

"Well, I think he must have a friend somewhere. He's started to run off, and we can't find out where he goes."

"We had a cat once named Fluffy," Ben said. "He did that. But now we got a dog named Spike."

Juliet found out that Ben played ball. She said, "Our homeschool kids have ball games all the time. Maybe you could come over and play with us next time you visit."

"Sure! I'd like that!" he said. He stroked the kitten. "I wish I could be homeschooled. I've always thought it would be fun, but Mama said we can't do it."

"Why don't both of you come with us to the park and play right now? It's just down the street from here."

"Hey, that sounds great!" Ben said. He went over to his mother. "Mom, would it be all right if we go down the street to play ball?"

"Oh, I'm afraid you might get lost!" his mother said.

"The park is right down this same street that the nursing home is on," Juliet said quickly. "When you get through visiting, you can come down and pick them up. Or we'll just come back."

"Why . . . all right. That would be fine, then."

"You just leave Boots with me," Mrs. Jones said.

"Will that be all right?"

"Of course it will!"

"He won't be too much trouble, will he?"

"Not in the least. We enjoy each other's company, don't we, Boots?"

Juliet left Boots on the old woman's lap, and the children started off. As they walked along, Juliet told her two new friends about the homeschool kids they would meet.

"You'll like them," Juliet said. "They're all real nice."

When they reached the playground, they

found that the girls were on the swings. The boys were kicking around a soccer ball.

"Hey, everybody, come here and meet our new friends! This is Ben and Lexy Jones. They've got the same name as I have, but they're no relation."

After she introduced everyone, Chili said, "You can be on my team, Ben. Have you played soccer before?"

"I'm not too good, but I like to play."

Delores Del Rio went over to Lexy. "Hello, Lexy," she said. "I'm glad you could visit."

"None of you have to go to school?" Lexy asked.

"Oh, yes, but we go to school at home."

"Wow, I wish I could do that," Lexy said with longing in her voice.

"We have to work pretty hard, though." Joe grinned at her. "My mom's harder than any teacher we ever had in public school."

Then Flash wheeled his chair around. "Let's get at it! We came here to play soccer!"

The game was soon going full speed ahead. It turned out that Ben was a good soccer player after all. And although Lexy was small, she was very fast and never seemed to get tired.

Then Juliet looked at her watch. "I expect we'd better get you two back to the nursing home."

"Oh, let's play just a little more," Ben said.

"Better not. It's time for Jenny and me to get home, so we have to go."

On the way back toward the nursing home, Ben said, "Do you suppose we can play with you guys again?"

"Sure. Anytime you're here visiting your grandmother. We come to the park almost every day after we've finished our lessons."

Lexy said. "We'll come over, then."

Juliet went in to pick up Boots. She said, "We have to go now, but we'll come back again."

Mrs. Jones stroked the cat's black fur lovingly. "I hate to see him go." She sighed. "He's such good company for me."

When they were outside again, Juliet said, "I always hate to take Boots away from Mrs. Jones. She enjoys him so much."

"Too bad she can't have a kitty of her own. But I guess if they ever let one person have a pet, everybody would want one."

Juliet played in the backyard with her kitten until the sun began to set. Supper was later than usual, but her mother had it almost ready. Boots was sitting on her lap, and Juliet was stroking his fur.

Suddenly Boots jumped off and ran for the hedge.

"Boots, you come back here!" Juliet yelled. She scrambled up, ran around the end of the hedge, and began to call for him anxiously.

"Boots! Boots! You come back here! Oh, no! Not again!"

But it had happened again, just as it had happened before! Boots had disappeared, and she could not find him.

As she and Joe went upstairs to bed that night, he said, "I can't figure out where that cat is going."

"I can't either. I guess he just likes to roam."

"Well, he'll probably be back in the morning again," Joe said. "I know you worry about him, but it'll be OK. He'll come back."

Juliet was glad that Joe was so kind, but she still felt bad about Boots.

When she got to her room, she just sat on her bed awhile, thinking about the cat. Then she got up and stood at the window for a long time.

Finally she said, "Well, I guess there's nothing I can do until tomorrow."

As usual before climbing into bed, Juliet said her prayers for people and things that she was concerned about. She prayed a special prayer for Boots. "Oh, Lord. Don't let anything happen to him and bring him back safe."

After she had prayed, she felt better. The last thing she thought before dropping off to sleep was *I'll bet he'll be at the back door when I get up in the morning.*

A Chain of Daisies

When Juliet woke up the next morning, the first thing she thought was *I'll bet Boots is at the back door.* She jumped out of bed, pulled on her robe and slippers, and then—as quietly as she could—went downstairs. It was barely dawn, and she didn't want to wake up any of the family.

She went through the downstairs on tiptoe and opened the back door. She stepped out eagerly onto the porch and looked around—but then her heart dropped.

"Boots, you're not here!" she spoke aloud. She was so disappointed that she wanted to cry.

Maybe he's out by the storage shed, she thought next. *He crawls under it sometimes.*

She walked around the backyard, calling quietly, "Come here, kitty, kitty, kitty! Here,

Boots!" But no Boots appeared. Then she sat on the back steps until the sun was over the horizon, hoping that he would come back.

"Juliet, whatever are you doing out here?"

Turning around, Juliet saw her mother standing at the open door.

"I came out to see if Boots was here."

"He's not?"

"No. He's not here. Oh, Mom, what's happened to him?"

"Probably nothing. He's just one of those cats that likes to wander," Mrs. Jones said. "I once had two kittens at the same time. One of them would never even leave the house. He was just a house kitty. But the other was a wanderer. He went all over town. He always came back, though. Come on in and help me fix breakfast."

Juliet got up and went inside. After getting dressed, she helped her mother.

Dad and Joe came down then, and they all sat down at the table. As usual, they held hands while they said the blessing. Her dad prayed, "Lord, thanks for the food," and then said, "And we do ask that You bring Boots back. We know You're able to do all things, and this cat is very important to Juliet. So I pray that You will bring him back safely."

"Amen!" Joe said and began to fill his plate with scrambled eggs. He took a huge bite of egg, then a bite out of a biscuit.

"Joe, I've told you not to take such big bites!" his mother scolded.

"But, Mom," Joe said, smiling and talking around the food in his mouth, "you cook so good."

"Never mind all that. Flattery doesn't make up for bad manners."

"Well, it's Saturday," Mr. Jones said. "What are you two going to do today?"

"We're going over to play with our new friends this afternoon," Joe said. "They're here for a few days, visiting their grandmother. They're pretty neat. Especially Ben. He's a great soccer player."

"And Lexy's nice, too. I like her a lot," Juliet said.

"I remember when I was your age," their father said, as he put butter and strawberry jam on a hot biscuit. "Saturday was the best day in the week. I lived all five days just to get to Saturday and Sunday."

"I guess all boys and girls are like that," Mrs. Jones said. "Except for summertime, when you youngsters don't have to go to school. Then every day's nice."

"I'll be glad when it's summer." Joe finished off a huge glass of milk. "Juliet, don't worry. There's plenty more cats if you lose that one."

"Don't talk that way!" she cried.

"Aw, I was just mouthing off. Don't pay any attention to me." Sometimes Joe teased his sister when it was not entirely the right thing to do. Now he did seem to feel sorry about what he'd said. "He'll be OK."

"Mom, can I go out and look for Boots?"

"Yes, and you go with her, Joe."

As they left the house, Joe suggested, "Let's look over on Pine Court."

They walked down the street. The sun was shining brightly now, and they stopped at several houses where neighbors were already out in their yards. They asked if anyone had seen a black kitten with white feet. But all the neighbors said no.

They called as they went, and once Joe said, "I sure feel silly saying, 'Kitty, kitty, kitty.' He's almost a full-grown cat, but you can't go around calling, 'Here, cat—here, cat—here, cat.'"

Juliet stopped to look in a yard surrounded by a hedge. She hoped to catch sight of black-and-white fur, but she saw nothing. "We might as well go home, Joe," she said sadly.

"All right. I want to do some work on my new invention, anyway." Joe was always inventing things. His latest was an intercom system for the house. So far it had not worked, but he had insisted that it would, as soon as he got enough parts.

The rest of the morning, Juliet helped her mother and read, while Joe worked on the intercom system. At the same time Juliet was working or reading, in the back of her mind she was listening for a tiny *"Mrow."*

That afternoon Juliet and Joe went off to meet Ben and Lexy. They met at the ice cream shop, where each of them had a soft drink. Then they went to the mall.

The mall was not as big as some in larger cities, but Juliet and Joe liked to go there. They each liked to do different things in the mall, however.

Joe said, "I'm not going to look at any old clothes! Come on, Ben. Let's go over to the arcade."

"That sounds good to me," Ben said cheerfully. "I've been saving up some money."

"When will we meet?" Juliet asked. "And where?"

"Aw, after you get through looking at every dress and pair of shoes in the mall, just come over to the arcade. We'll be there."

At the arcade, the boys immediately began playing.

"My folks won't let me play this game much," Ben said.

"Why not?"

"Well, it's all about cars crashing into buildings and into trees and stuff. They're afraid it'll be a bad influence."

"It's just a game!" Joe said with surprise.

"I know, but my folks say it could put some bad driving habits in me."

"I don't think so. My dad likes to play, and he's the most careful driver I know."

As soon as the boys went off to the arcade, Juliet and Lexy began walking around. "I don't want to buy anything, really," Juliet said. "I just like to look."

"Me too. Sometimes my mom brings me to the mall, and we look all afternoon and don't buy anything."

They looked in the windows of store after store. After a while, Juliet said, "I'm getting hungry. Let's find Joe and Ben and get something to eat."

They found the boys just standing and watching others play. "I'm starved," Juliet said.

"I don't have any money," Joe complained. "We spent it all on games."

She laughed. "I ought to let you go hungry, but I've got enough to buy us both something. The treat's on me." Then she said, "I'll tell you what. Let's get some of those big pretzels. Does everyone like them?" She knew Joe did, and it turned out that Ben and Lexy liked them, too. "Let's all get one and get different toppings."

"Hey, that's cool!" Joe said. "I want mustard on mine."

"I want chocolate on mine," Lexy said.

"Chocolate! That's no good!" Ben said. "I want nacho cheese."

"And that sounds awful!" Juliet said. She studied the menu. "I think I'll have strawberry cream cheese."

They ordered their pretzels and then took them over to a table. Juliet was eating hers when Joe suddenly dipped his finger in his topping and put some right on the tip of her nose.

"Joe, what a mess!" she cried.

Ben took a little of his topping and put it on Lexy's face.

They were giggling and making a lot of noise when Juliet saw Flash Gordon and Chili Williams.

"Hey, Flash—Chili! Come over here!"

Flash wheeled over in his chair. Chili walked beside him, dribbling a basketball. Chili was wearing the most violent colored green shirt that Juliet had ever seen.

"Wow, that makes my eyes hurt!" Joe said. "Where'd you get it, Chili?"

"Bought it at a store that sells fine clothes. You just wish you had it, don't you?"

Flash said, "Let's us get some pretzels, too. I think I'll have one with cheese."

The six of them had a good time at the pretzel booth, but after a while Juliet said, "Let's go walk around the mall a little bit more."

There were lots of other boys and girls there, and she knew most of them. She kept watching Chili dribble his basketball. He was good. He could dribble with either hand, behind his back, and between his legs. He could spin the ball on his uplifted fingers, too.

And Flash Gordon was good with his wheelchair. As he moved around, he was careful not to bump into anybody. He handled it very well.

Once, when the boys had gotten ahead of them, Lexy said, "It's too bad that Flash has to be in a wheelchair."

"Yes, it is. But he says the Lord's going to make him well someday."

"I hope He does. That would be wonderful."

When everybody was about to start for home, Ben said, "This was more fun than anything I've done in a long time."

"Let's do it again before you have to go home."

And then they said their good-byes.

That night at dinner, Juliet and Joe talked about Lexy and Ben. They told their parents all that they had done.

Their mother said, "I'm just not sure about your spending so much time at that mall."

"Oh, we didn't spend much money!" Joe protested. "Just a few arcade games and some pretzels!"

After supper Juliet and Joe watched a special on TV. It was about building the pyramids, and Joe was fascinated. "Wow, I wish I could have been there and helped build those things."

Juliet laughed. "You wouldn't be here now if you were there then."

"Sure I would. I'd just be five thousand years old."

At bedtime, Juliet looked outside to check for Boots one more time. She called him softly, but he did not come.

After she had taken her shower and gone to bed, she read for a long time because she was not sleepy. As she was reading, a thought came to her. *I'm just going to look one more time for Boots.* She went downstairs and without much hope opened the back door—and there he was!

"Boots!" She swooped him up and danced around the kitchen, not caring if she woke everybody up. He said, *"Mrow!"* to Juliet and licked her chin. Then she noticed that he had a delicate necklace of wildflowers around his neck.

She took off the flower necklace and turned it around in her fingers. "I wonder where in the world you could have gotten this. Somebody made it."

Boots said, *"Mrow!"*

"I'll bet you're hungry." She put him down

and took out some tuna cat food, which he always liked. She put it on the floor.

Boots sniffed at it and then walked away.

"You're not even hungry, are you?"

Puzzled, she picked him up again and took him upstairs to bed with her. When she lay down, he plopped himself down on the pillow beside her head as he always did. She stroked his silky fur and said, "I wish you could talk and could tell me where you've been."

Boots yawned hugely, showing his white teeth.

"You are a naughty kitty!"

Boots said, *"Mrow!"* Then he tucked his head under Juliet's arm and went to sleep.

She sighed. "Well, I can see you're really shook up about being such a terrible bother!"

The Blue Booties

When the Joneses approached the front door of the church, Juliet saw Lexy and Ben with their parents.

"Look," she said, "those are the kids we told you about. The ones we met at the nursing home."

"Well, we'd better meet their parents. I believe they're first-time visitors," her dad said.

And soon Mr. and Mrs. Jones were introduced to Mr. and Mrs. Jones. Ben and Lexy's father was a big man with light hair. Their mother was small and dark.

"We're glad you're visiting our church," Juliet told Ben and Lexy. "Sunday school's about ready to start. You can be in our class."

Juliet and Joe led their new friends down the hall. When they walked into the classroom, the teacher, Mr. Blanton, looked up with a smile. "Well, we have some more visitors to-day!"

"Yes, and their name is Jones, too. This is Lexy, and this is Ben."

"Oh, are they relatives of yours?"

"No. We're not related, but there are a lot of Joneses in the world."

"Too many of them, if you ask me!"

Juliet looked and saw that it was Billy Rollins talking. He did not usually attend their church, but he sometimes visited with Jack Tanner, who did. Behind Billy were Helen and Ray Boyd. They were identical twins and were almost as spoiled as Billy Rollins. The three of them usually got together.

Jack muttered, "Aw, don't talk like that, Billy." He was a thin boy with light brown hair and blue eyes.

But Juliet knew Billy Rollins always talked like that. She rolled her eyes and muttered to Jenny, "Oh, no, we've got to put up with *him* again!"

Billy overheard this. "You're not supposed to talk in class," he said loudly.

"Why don't you introduce your new friends to us all," Mr. Blanton said, and the children quieted down.

"This is Ben and Lexy Jones," Juliet repeated. "They're just visiting, but I made a good friend out of their grandmother. You remember. We saw her at the nursing home."

Most of the class said they did remember Mrs. Eliza Jones, which seemed to make Ben and Lexy feel good.

Mr. Blanton let them talk for a while, then said, "All right. Now we'll begin the lesson. If you'll all sit down, we'll get started."

There was the usual scrambling for chairs. Juliet sat between Ben and Lexy. She whispered, "Mr. Blanton's really a good Sunday school teacher."

The lesson that morning was on being kind, and Mr. Blanton did, indeed, do a good job. He had not gotten far, though, before Billy Rollins said loudly, "Why do we have to study this? I'm always kind."

Most of the class laughed.

"Kind!" Joe said. "You're not kind!"

"Who's not kind?" Billy asked indignantly. "I'm always kind, aren't I?" He turned to the Boyd twins.

They both nodded. Ray said, "Sure, he's kind, and so are we."

Mr. Blanton smiled, and Juliet guessed that he understood Billy Rollins. "Sometimes we're unkind and we don't even realize it," he said, looking straight at Billy. He then began to talk about how important it was to always think what our words would do. "The Bible says that it's possible to speak a word that is like the piercing of a sword. What do you suppose that means?"

"I know," Juliet said. "I've had people say sharp things to me, and that's exactly what it felt like. Just like getting stuck with a sword."

"Yeah," Jack Tanner said. "When people call me skinny, it hurts."

"Words *can* hurt," Mr. Blanton said, "so we need to be very careful what we say. But another Bible verse says that a good word spoken at the right time is very good."

"I know what that's like," Jenny said. "I feel bad sometimes, and then Juliet comes up and says how pretty my hair looks or something, and it makes me feel better."

Billy sat listening to all this. But he said, "Well, I don't think I've ever said anything bad to anybody."

Juliet was suddenly tired of him. "Billy, you keep calling me 'Too Smart Jones,' and you know how I don't like it."

Billy appeared to be surprised. "Why, I thought you'd like it! Everybody wants to be smart."

"You *know* I don't like it, Billy."

After Sunday school, Lexy asked, "What was that 'Too Smart Jones' all about?"

Juliet hesitated. "I always made good grades, and in the town where we lived they started calling me that. I always hated it. When we moved here, I decided I didn't want to be called that anymore, so I decided to be dumb."

Both Ben and Lexy looked at her. "How can anybody decide to be dumb?"

"I mean I pretended to be dumb," Juliet said as they walked down the hall toward the auditorium. "I even failed tests on purpose just to make bad grades. I felt bad about doing that after a while and quit. I was trying to be something I'm not, and I think we ought to be what we are. But you don't know how bad I hate that nickname."

"Do kids here call you that?"

"Some of them do. Like Billy and the Boyd twins. Billy especially. When they found out about the nickname, they started to use it. I just have to put up with it."

The four found seats with their parents for the church service.

Jenny was sitting right in front of Juliet. Once she turned around and made a face. But her mother whispered, "Jenny, if you don't turn around and be still, I'm going to pinch you!"

Juliet silently giggled and was given "the look" by her mother.

By the time church started, everyone had settled down. Juliet loved to sing, although she didn't have a very good voice. She could hear Jenny and wished that she could sing as well as Jenny could. *I'd rather be able to sing like that than be smart,* she thought.

Juliet and her family went home after

church to a delicious dinner of baked ham, green bean casserole, baked potatoes, and applesauce cake.

After the dishes were washed, she noticed Boots standing at the back door. He meowed until she let him out. She watched rather sadly as he made straight for the hedge. "Well, I guess he's just going to be a wandering cat, and there's nothing I can do about it. I just have to trust the Lord even about my cat—to bring him back safe."

She went upstairs to listen to her CD player for a while. She put on headphones so that she wouldn't disturb anybody. Lying on her bed, listening to the music, and knowing nobody could hear it but herself—all of that gave her a nice sense of privacy. All the time she was listening, though, she was thinking, *I wonder where Boots goes to. If I'm as smart as they say I am, I could figure out where he goes. It's another big mystery to be solved.*

Then Juliet started trying to think of ways to follow Boots or to trace him. And finally she dozed off.

She woke up with a start, for Joe was yelling, "Come on! Come on! Get out of that bed! Quit listening to that dumb music!"

"It's not dumb music!" But Juliet got up. Then she saw with a shock that she had been asleep for a whole hour!

She and Joe went downstairs and got out

their bicycles as they usually did on Sunday afternoons. They rode along their quiet street, racing and doing stunts. Both were expert bicycle riders. They were about to turn onto Elm Street when suddenly Joe shouted, "Look! There's Boots!"

Juliet looked and caught just a glimpse of her cat sauntering through the park. They jumped off their bicycles, lay them down under a tree, and started for the woods.

But Boots seemed to know that he was being chased. He ran like a black flash, and the two lost sight of him.

"I don't know what's with that cat," Joe panted. "What's he up to? Why don't you solve this mystery?"

"That's just what I was thinking while I was napping."

"You can think while you're taking a nap? I can't even think when I'm not taking a nap." He looked around them. "We aren't going to find that cat."

"I guess not."

They gave up and headed back to their bikes.

When they got home that afternoon, Juliet told their parents about seeing Boots in the park.

Her dad said, "He's a mystery cat, all right."

"He sure is," her mother added. "But he seems able to take care of himself."

After supper, they watched Billy Graham on television. And then Mrs. Jones said, "You two better go to bed early tonight. The Support Group outing is tomorrow, as I'm sure you haven't forgotten."

"All right, Mom," both said and went upstairs.

Juliet was ready for bed when Joe suddenly knocked on her door. "Hey, I was downstairs getting a glass of milk, and *Boots* was at the door. I let him in."

"He's back?" Juliet ran down, and sure enough there in the kitchen was Boots, just as before. He meowed, and she picked him up.

"What in the world is this on your feet?"

Somebody had put four little knitted baby booties on his paws. They were fastened on with small rubber bands, and Boots apparently had been unable to get them off.

"Well, that's something!" Joe spoke behind her. "Who in the world would put socks on a cat?"

"I don't know, but I'm going to find out somehow or other!" Juliet said with determination.

She tried to feed Boots, but again he was not hungry after his travels. She took him upstairs, removed the tiny boots, and stared at them for a long time. "Blue booties on a cat. I can't figure this out. I'm going to have to be a better detective than I have been to find out what you do on your adventures, Boots."

Boots looked at her, yawned, and said, *"Mrow!"*

"I wish you'd learn to say something else." Then Juliet picked him up and hugged him. "But I'm glad you're back." The cat struggled to get loose, but she held him fast. "Maybe I'll get a parrot, and then he can say something besides '*Mrow!*'"

Boots licked her face. Then he yawned hugely, cuddled up, and went to sleep.

Television Stars

As usual when the Oakwood Support Group met at the church, there was much loud talk and playing around. Today the boys and girls were all excited about their new project, and the parents were trying to get them into order.

"I'm really excited about this," Joe said, his eyes shining. "We've had some dumb projects before—like going to the canning factory to see how they canned peaches."

"Oh, I liked that!" Juliet exclaimed. "I thought it was interesting!"

"Well, I didn't think so!" Joe said with disgust. Then his eyes brightened again. "But to get to go to a TV station and find out how to read a weather map and how they do all that stuff we see on television—that's really fun." He jumped up and down.

"Maybe they'll let us be on TV," Chili Williams said.

"That sounds good," Billy Rollins answered. He stuck out his chest and walked around trying to look important. "I'd make a great newsman. Here—this is me being a news reporter."

Juliet watched Billy give his impersonation of a newscaster. Then she said, "You're going to have to learn how to use better English if you're going to do that job."

"Who says so?"

"I say so," Juliet said. "You use terrible grammar. You say 'ain't' all the time."

"There's nothing wrong with saying 'ain't.' It's in the dictionary."

"The dictionary says it's 'substandard English.' That means it's not the best English."

"Well, I'll be so charming that people won't care whether I say 'ain't.'"

Jack Tanner's dad, who was going to take them to the station, said, "Listen up, now!" He waited for quiet. He was a very tall man and thin, with crisp brown hair and blue eyes. He wore thick glasses and was a writer, and Juliet thought he knew most everything.

"You're going to have to behave yourselves when we get to the studio. They've been very nice to let us come, so we're going to be on our best behavior. Right?"

"Right!" Flash Gordon called out from his

wheelchair. "The rest of you just watch me and do like I do. Then you'll be all right."

A laugh went around the room, and Samuel Del Rio nudged his sister, Delores. "Just watch us," he said. "Maybe we'll do a couple of back flips just to get attention. Maybe they'll let us do some on TV!" The Del Rios were the children of circus performers and could, indeed, do back flips.

"You'd better save the back flips for some other time," Mr. Tanner said. He put a hand on Jack's shoulder and said, "I'll watch this one." He put his other hand on the shoulder of Jenny, his stepdaughter, and said, "And I'll watch this one too."

Jenny said, "I always behave. You don't have to watch me, Dad."

"Just remember—everybody—we all have to be on our best behavior. We can't get in the way of the television people."

Juliet's parents had invited Ben and Lexy to come, too. Now Lexy came over to Juliet, her eyes bright. She said, "I'm so excited!"

"Me too! You stay with me, and you too, Ben."

"Do you think we'll get to see any celebrities?" Ben asked.

"Maybe there'll be some there," Jenny said. "Wouldn't that be fun! I'm going to get their autographs."

On the way to the studio, Juliet told Jenny

and Lexy about her cat's latest adventure. She ended the story with her most interesting news: "And he came back this time wearing blue booties just like a baby wears."

"Oh, you're kidding me!" Jenny protested.

"I'm not! He really had them on!"

"Cats don't keep anything on their feet!" Jenny argued. "I tried to put some on one of my cats one time. He had a fit."

"Well, these were fastened on with rubber bands, and I guess he couldn't get them off."

"Who do you think put them on?" Lexy asked.

"I don't know, and I wish I did. It's a mystery. He runs off every night, and we just don't know where he goes."

"Why don't you follow him?"

"We've tried to, but have you ever tried to keep up with a cat in the woods? He's so fast! Joe and I have lost him every time."

"It's funny to have a cat wearing booties."

"He looked so cute in them." Juliet laughed. "I put them on him sometimes. He doesn't seem to mind them anymore." She thought for a while and nodded. "I'm going to find out where he's going. You see if I don't!"

They arrived at the television studio, and Jack Tanner's dad led them in. There they met a short man who said his name was Williams.

"Mr. Williams is the manager here at the station, kids," Mr. Tanner explained. "We appreciate his letting us come and see how a TV station works, don't we?"

Mr. Williams grinned at the chorus of yeses that went up. "We're glad to have you here, kids. It's a little crowded—we're not a big station—but you just try not to get run over by a camera or something."

Billy Rollins said, "What's the chance of getting on a TV show, Mr. Williams?"

"And do what?"

"Oh, I can do lots of things. I can imitate birds, for one thing."

"Well, the next time we have an amateur hour—" Mr. Williams grinned "—we'll give you a shot at it. Now, come along, and I'll give you a quick walk-through."

Chili said, "I can imitate a chicken."

Mr. Williams laughed. "Lots of people can do that."

"Not like I do it!"

"How do *you* imitate a chicken?"

Chili grinned. "I eat a worm!"

Everyone laughed, but Mr. Williams said, "Sorry. I think we'd get unhappy letters from our viewers if you did that!"

For the next thirty minutes, Mr. Williams showed them how reporters did their jobs, how to read a weather map, and where the meteorologists got their information from what he called Doppler radar.

Joe asked so many questions that finally

Juliet pulled at his sleeve. “Don’t talk so much! Mr. Williams won’t like it.”

“Why, I don’t mind at all,” the station manager said, looking with approval at Joe. “That’s a bright young fellow there. He learns by asking questions.”

Flash Gordon was taking it all in, too. At times it was really hard to remember that he could not walk. He moved his wheelchair so well. And in the studio he was everywhere, looking and learning.

Juliet was watching when Flash wheeled himself up to two of the reporters. “Hi,” he said. “My name’s Flash.”

The man and the woman both grinned and told him their names—Harry and Jane.

Flash said, “Can you teach us about how to give a weather report?”

“Well, why don’t *you* practice giving the weather report?” Harry said. “Here, come over in front of this screen.”

“But there’s nothing on it,” Flash said.

“There never is. When we’re standing in front of these screens to give the weather report, they’re blank.”

“But I see you pointing to different places,” Flash argued.

“But we’re looking at a monitor over there while we talk. See? There are several of them.”

“Well, why don’t you just put the weather stuff on the screen?”

"Because it would be too hard for us to keep our eye on the screen and on the camera at the same time. This way, we can look at the camera while another camera shows what's on the screen. Now, you try it."

Flash grinned. "I'll try anything," he said. "Except boiled okra. I tried that once, and it was no good."

As everyone stood around watching, Juliet said to Jenny, "Boy, he's got a lot of nerve to do that."

"I don't believe he'd be afraid to try anything."

The reporter called Harry put Flash in position and showed him the monitor that showed the weather map. "Now you just talk and tell us what's coming in."

Flash grinned and looked into the camera. Right away, Juliet saw, he discovered how to point to the right place.

"Well, right here we have heavy rains coming in along the Seattle, Washington, area"—he pointed to the map—"and we have a cold front coming down from Canada. You see those big clouds there? It's going to be a cold one, folks. Get your snow shovels out.

"And down on the Gulf Coast, a hurricane is kicking up in the Caribbean. Better get ready. Looks like it's going to be a bad one."

Everyone applauded Flash's weather report.

When he asked, "How's that?" Harry said, "I'll ask to have you put on the payroll. You did a great job."

"Really? Well, maybe I'd better learn more about the weather. I might want to do this when I grow up."

Mr. Williams had been watching, too. He said, "We've got plenty of time here. Why don't each of you try it? Who knows? The best future weatherman or weatherwoman in America might be right here."

So each homeschooler got to stand in front of the blank map and make up weather reports. It was a fun afternoon. When the visit was over, they all went by and thanked Mr. Williams.

"It was great, Mr. Williams," Joe said. "I'm kind of a scientist myself."

"Really! Well, you'll have to come by and help us on some of these technical things." Mr. Williams grinned and winked. Then he said, "Seriously, we're glad to have you boys and girls visit us. I hope that some of you will be working someday in a studio just like this."

All the way back to the church where they had their large group meetings, they chattered and talked and pretended they were TV personalities.

"We didn't see any celebrities," Jenny said, "but it was fun."

"Yes, it was," Juliet said. "It's funny to

think of a time when there was no TV. I guess people just listened to the radio back then. My grandmother tells me about it sometimes."

"My grandmother told me," Chili said, "that when she was a girl they didn't even have a radio. They lived on a farm and didn't have any electricity."

"That would be terrible! No fridge, no electric lights."

"They had to use lanterns and things like that. I guess we're not grateful enough for the good things we have."

When they were back and unloaded, Juliet said, "Let's go down to the ice cream parlor."

"Sounds like a winner to me!" Lexy said. "I like ice cream."

Joe, Ben, Jenny, Samuel, and Delores decided to join them. All seven talked about nothing but television all the way there.

It took a while for them to choose what ice cream they wanted. Joe wanted nothing but vanilla, Juliet liked pistachio, Jenny got chocolate, Ben strawberry, Lexy caramel, Delores lime, and Samuel would have nothing but a double, extra large rocky road.

They sat at a table, licking their cones and making them last as long as they could.

They talked about the outing for a while longer, and then Joe winked at Samuel. "Hey, Sam! You know how some people can't keep any friends?"

"So I hear," Sam said, as though he knew that Joe was going to tease somebody.

"Well, let me tell you about somebody that can't even keep a cat for a friend."

"Joe, don't you start!" Juliet warned.

"I'm not starting! I'm just telling the truth! Juliet's got this cat and does everything for him, and he just leaves home every day and won't come back till he's ready."

"He just wanders," Juliet said. "That's all."

Lexy said, "Joe, don't tease her about it. She doesn't like it."

"She'll get used to it! Why, that cat has probably found somebody that treats him right."

Juliet got up. "I'm leaving! I don't want to listen to this."

"Now, see what you did, Joe! You hurt her feelings," Lexy said, as Juliet made for the door.

"Oh, she's always getting her feelings hurt!"

Delores and Lexy caught up with Juliet at the corner.

"I'm sorry he was so mean—and your own brother, too," Lexy said.

"Oh, I know he doesn't really mean it. Brothers are just like that. They like to tease," Juliet said.

"Let's go to the park! The flowers are so pretty," Delores suggested.

"That sounds good to me," Juliet agreed.

At the park, the girls walked by the pond. They laughed when the ducks stuck their heads under the water and turned their bottoms up. Then they waddled up to the girls, quacking, and Juliet had to say, "Nothing for you today."

"I bring bread for them sometimes," Delores said. "They love it."

They walked around the pond, trying to see fish but did not see any. They did see one turtle. He was sunning himself on a log but went splashing in when he heard the girls coming.

Then they went strolling along a brick walk, and suddenly Juliet said, "Look there!"

"What is it?" Lexy asked.

"It's this!" She bent over and picked up a necklace made out of clover flowers. "This is just like the one Boots came home wearing!" she exclaimed. "I wonder if whoever put it on him made this one?"

"I doubt it," Lexy said. "Lots of people make those. I make them myself."

"Let's make some right now," Delores said.

So they sat in the grass and made enough fragile flower necklaces to go around their necks several times.

"I'm sorry you and Ben have to go home tomorrow, Lexy."

"Me too. We've had such a good time here. I really like my grandmother, and we'll miss all of you a lot."

"Maybe you can visit us the next time you come to see her."

"I hope so," Lexy said. "Sometimes we have more fun here than we do at home."

They wandered along the winding brick walk that meandered through the park. They went down a steep hill to the stream and then threw pebbles into it for a while. Finally Juliet sighed. "I guess it's time to go home. It sure has been a good day."

"Sure has," Delores agreed. "Never thought I'd get to be a TV star."

"I think Flash was the best. He's a good announcer. Maybe he'll be rich and famous someday, and we can say we knew him before he got that way."

They then wandered on toward home.

When Juliet reached the house, Joe met her by the front walk. "Hi, Juliet." He seemed embarrassed. He scuffed his toe in the grass. "I'm sorry. I didn't mean to hurt your feelings."

"Oh, it's all right, Joe. I do the same to you sometimes. Let's go in and eat supper."

"That's always a good idea!"

"If it involves eating, you think it's a good idea."

"Eating supper was *your* idea."

"Well, a person's got to eat to live."

"Can't think of a better reason right now! Let's go!"

Following Boots

Juliet sat on the front steps playing with Boots. She laughed when he jumped as high as he could to catch the ribbon that she dangled for him. He was a very active cat. Juliet said, “If a circus acrobat was as good as you, he’d sure be famous!”

She admired the way the cat could jump straight up in the air, twist himself around, catch the ribbon, and then fall on all four feet. “I bet you could turn a back flip if you wanted to.” She dragged the ribbon across the ground. He twitched his tail, and his eyes were bright. Then he pounced on it, fell on his back, and held it with his hind claws.

“You’re the best cat in all the world, Boots!” Juliet said. “I have more fun with you than you can imagine.”

Boots looked up. He said, *"Mrow!"* Then he kept on trying to destroy the ribbon.

Juliet was still playing with Boots when a car rolled up the driveway. "Come on, Boots. It's Dad." She ran to meet her father.

When he got out of the car, he gave her a big hug. "What's my girl been doing all day? Playing with that cat?"

"Most of the time. What have you been doing, Dad?"

Mr. Jones wiped his forehead with his sleeve. He looked hot. "I've been building a bridge across a creek over at the other end of the county."

"Can I go with you sometime and watch you?"

"Sure. You and Joe both can go. Even Boots, if you want to take him."

"Oh, that would be fun! Maybe that can be our next project—watching a bridge get built."

"It's a pretty hot project, but I'd be glad to have you. Maybe your mother would want to come and bring a lunch. We could make a picnic out of it. I'll work, and you watch. Then we'll all eat. What's Joe been doing?"

"He's working on his new invention."

"You mean the intercom system?"

"Oh, no. He's off on something new. He's making a rocket."

"Going to the moon, is he?" Mr. Jones smiled. "He's always building something."

"It's just a little rocket, but it's supposed to go way up in the air. Probably will come down on our heads." Juliet made a face.

"Well, that sounds like fun. I'll bet it'll work, too. Joe's getting pretty good at making things."

They sat down together on the back steps and watched the sun as it continued to go down. It was a huge yellow ball. Juliet thought she could almost see it move.

"That's a pretty sunset," she said.

"Sure is. God makes beautiful ones." Then Mr. Jones picked up Boots. "Still no idea about where this fellow goes every day?"

"Not a clue, Dad. He just disappears. I worry about him a lot. He could get run over or something."

"We'll hope for better things than that." For a while her father just rested and played with Boots.

Juliet said, "He's the most playful kitten. He'll play with anybody."

"He never meets a stranger, that's for sure."

"I've been trying to think about how to find out where he goes, Dad. Somebody's feeding him. He hardly eats a bite when he comes home."

"And somebody made these booties for him." Mr. Jones fingered one of the blue booties that Juliet had put on the cat's paws. "He didn't make them himself."

"They're pretty booties, too."

"They sure are. My grandmother—your great-grandmother—used to knit things like this. I had a pair of gloves that she made me. I never could see how anybody makes fingers on gloves."

"I'd like to learn to knit, too."

"I'll tell you what we'll do," Mr. Jones said. "After supper let's have your mother put Boots out the back door a few minutes after we leave by the front door. Then we'll sneak around and see where he goes."

"Hey, that sounds cool, Dad!" She reached up and hugged him. "Not many dads would take this much time for their daughters."

Mr. Jones hugged Juliet back. "You're my favorite daughter!"

"I'm your only daughter!"

"Then I guess that's why you're my favorite. Come on. Your mother probably has supper about ready."

All during supper, Joe talked about his new invention. It was going to go up a thousand feet, he said.

"And it'll probably smash our house when it falls." Juliet took another bite of the chocolate pie that her mother had made.

"Well, it won't!" Joe said indignantly. "It's got a parachute. When it gets up a thousand feet, the nose blows off and a parachute deploys."

"Deploys! Where are you getting those big words?" Juliet grinned at her father.

"I read about it in the *World Book Encyclopedia.* The parachute deploys. That means it pops out, and then the rocket just floats to the ground."

"Well, it won't kill us or smash our house if it's got a parachute," Juliet said.

"Sounds like fun. What makes the thing go up, Joe?" Mr. Jones asked.

"Oh, you can buy engines for them. It's really just a skyrocket. Would you like to come out and help me with it, Dad?"

"Sure. Next weekend we'll go out and rocket away. You may be on one of those things headed for the moon someday. Who knows? And"—he turned to Juliet—"your sister and I have a plan for solving the mystery of the wandering cat."

"How are you going to do that?" Mrs. Jones asked. She was sipping her coffee, and she lifted her eyebrows in a questioning look. "Nobody can keep up with that cat."

"We're going to sneak up on him," Mr. Jones said. "You're going to let him out the back door just a few minutes after we leave by the front door. Then we'll watch where he goes."

"He goes to that hedge, and then you have to run around it. That's what he does!" Joe said, eating his last bite of pie. “Can I have another piece of pie?”

“I guess so. If you have room for it,” his mother said.

“But it’ll be dark out there,” Joe said, back to thinking about the cat.

“No, we’ve got another hour of daylight. Let’s do it right now, Juliet,” Mr. Jones said.

“Now? But we’ve got to do the dishes now,” Juliet said.

“Look, we’ve got a mystery on our hands here.” Mr. Jones winked at her. “We’ve got to solve it, haven’t we, Too Smart?”

“Now, don’t you start, Dad. It’s bad enough when Billy Rollins calls me that.”

“OK. I’ll try to watch it. But it’s a pretty good nickname, I think. Are we all ready?”

“I guess so,” Juliet said. “Mom, we’ll go out the front door. Give us about two minutes. Then let Boots out the back door.”

“What do *I* do?” Joe asked.

“You wash the dishes,” his father answered.

“But I want to help!”

“Two of us can keep up with one little cat. You do the dishes. That will help. As soon as your mother lets the cat out, Juliet and I’ll be off and running.”

Joe protested that he deserved to go, too, but in the end that was the way they did it. Juliet and her dad went out the front door and made for the side of the house.

"We'll hide over by those bushes," he said. "That way we can cut around the hedge."

"He always goes through that hole in the hedge right there. But the branches are too thick for us to get through."

"If we were Olympic hurdlers, we could just jump the hedge," her father said. "But this time we'll just go around it."

"The back door's opening. There. Mom's putting Boots outside."

Boots came onto the porch. As soon as the door closed, he made a run for the hedge.

"Run! He's going to get ahead of us!" Juliet's father exclaimed. They ran around the hedge just in time to see Boots come through.

The cat took off. Juliet and her father took off right after him. They kept him in sight for some time. He went through several backyards. He just jumped over or went under the fences. But they had to go around.

Mr. Jones was panting. "This is hard work," he said. "Harder than building bridges."

"Come on, Dad, we can't lose him!"

They kept on chasing the black cat. It was getting darker now and harder to see. But they would catch sight of his white feet every now and then. And then they turned a corner, expecting to see him—but he was gone!

"Well, he's done it again," Juliet said, almost in tears. "There's just no way to follow that cat."

"Don't worry about it, Juliet. It was just an idea that didn't work. I have lots of them. He's probably got a girlfriend somewhere."

"Oh, you always say that."

"Or maybe he's gone to the mall. Maybe he likes to window-shop. You do."

Juliet thought that was funny. "I can't imagine a cat window-shopping."

"Well, with Boots it might be birds, or squirrels, or maybe butterflies that he likes to see instead of clothes," her father said. "We might as well go home. He'll be back in the morning. He always is."

They reached the Jones house, and Juliet went upstairs. She was still trying to think of some way to keep track of Boots. She opened her diary and wrote:

> My dad and I tried to follow Boots to find out where he goes. But we lost him. Cats just like to roam, I guess. That's the way they are. But I get worried that he might get hit by a car. Somehow I'm going to solve this mystery. It was nice of Dad to help me, though.

Juliet went to bed but could not sleep. She stayed awake until eleven o'clock, tossing and turning. Finally she did drift off, but her sleep was not sound. She had a strange dream.

In the dream she was running through a

beautiful field full of flowers. She saw a brook with ducks and fish and a turtle in it. And every once in a while she saw a black cat wearing blue booties. It would hide behind trees.

When Juliet woke up, she whispered, "I'm not only thinking about Boots when I'm awake, but now I'm dreaming about him."

More Mystery

Juliet was running through a field of wildflowers. This time the flowers were all tying themselves into chains. They came and draped themselves around her neck. She was smelling their sweet fragrance when all of a sudden she woke up.

"I must have dreamed about flowers all night long again," she said to herself. "It was a good dream, but . . ." She remembered dreaming about Boots several times.

She put on a pair of jeans and a blue shirt that buttoned down the front. She had some new Dr. Marten shoes that she liked very much. She stood looking down and admiring them. She walked back and forth and thought of how much Delores and Jenny and the other girls would like them. Everybody wanted Dr. Marten shoes.

Then she brushed her hair. She thought, *I guess Boots is downstairs now. He always is. Every morning.* Still, she always felt a little worried until she saw him there.

Juliet hurried down the stairs. She saw that her mother was cooking pancakes, and she said, "Mom, I'll help you as soon as I check on Boots."

"Oh, I have breakfast about ready. And the cat's out there. I saw him playing in the apple tree."

Juliet looked out the window and saw Boots in the tree. The Joneses had a very nice backyard. There were several bird feeders. Even now some cardinals were pecking at the sunflower seed. Little yellow birds were eating over at another feeder. They looked almost like the canaries in the pet stores. She admired two lime green birds for a while. Juliet liked birds. In fact, she wanted a pet bird. But her father had said, "Why do you want to keep one inside when you have such nice ones outside? They enjoy that a lot more than being in a cage."

"I guess Boots doesn't have any new mittens on. I expect him to come back wearing shoes someday," she said.

Juliet's mother laughed. "That cat is certainly a mystery cat! I never heard of one like him. Imagine—going off and coming back with necklaces on and wearing booties."

"He is a fun kitty, but I wish he would stay home more," Juliet said. "I'll go out and get him. Maybe he'll be hungry."

However, she had difficulty even getting Boots to come down from the tree. He just sat up there and looked at her when she called.

"You're a naughty cat!" Juliet said. "Who do you think you are? The Cheshire cat in *Alice in Wonderland?*"

And then to her surprise Boots did seem to grin.

"Why, you *are* like the Cheshire cat!" she exclaimed. "Come on, now. Come down from there. You've had your fun."

Suddenly Boots gave a big leap, and she caught him in midair. "Now," she said, smoothing his fur, "come inside." She took him into the kitchen and poured him some milk.

But Boots just sniffed and turned up his nose at it.

"He doesn't eat anything much at all, Mom," Juliet said. "Somebody *has* to be feeding him."

"I don't know who'd do that," Mrs. Jones said, looking thoughtfully at the black cat with the beautiful white feet. "Most people don't feed strange cats."

"You do, Mom."

"I do once in a while when one seems real hungry. But Boots is so well fed and his fur's so sleek, anybody could take one look at him and know that he's getting plenty to eat."

"Well, I'm going to keep on trying to solve the mystery."

After breakfast she went up to begin her studies, taking Boots with her. He curled up next to her desk and went right to sleep.

Juliet watched him for a while and said to herself, "He sure is a nice kitty, but he is a pain in the neck, too. I don't know how you can get a kitty with a guarantee not to run off."

Over the next few weeks, Boots disappeared almost every night. Each time he would come home happy and fed. Once he came home with his fur especially smooth and shiny. It looked to Juliet as if someone had been brushing him.

Joe came to look. "Now who would have done that?" he said.

"I don't know. It's real strange. Why brush somebody else's cat?"

The next morning Joe discovered something else. He'd gone outside when he heard Boots meowing and came back holding the cat. "Look at this cat!" he said. He held him up.

Juliet asked, "What is it?"

"Well, look at his claws."

Juliet looked closer and gasped, "Why, somebody's put fingernail polish on them!"

"A cat with pink fingernails!"

"They're not fingernails! They're claws. But they are pink. Mom, look here!"

Mrs. Jones took one look and started laughing. "It looks like Boots has been to the beauty shop and gotten a manicure."

"I never saw such a thing," Joe said. "Imagine trying to paint a cat's toenails. They don't *like* people fooling with their feet."

"They sure don't, and Boots is worse than most," Juliet said. "It took somebody with a lot of patience to do that. Look how neatly it was done. Better than mine look when Mom lets me put on nail polish."

"Well, he didn't have to put it on himself," Joe said. "Somebody did it for him."

Two days later Boots came home with a blue bow around his neck. The following morning he had a small blue handkerchief tied around his neck like a cowboy.

"I don't know who's doing all this," Juliet said, "but it's awfully strange."

"It's someone who loves cats," her mother said. "That's very obvious."

"Maybe we could put an ad in the paper and ask who's feeding our cat and painting his claws."

"Yeah, you might do that, but it'll cost money," Joe said.

Juliet decided to write a story about her cat. She called it *The Adventures of Boots*. Every day she wrote down in a notebook whatever Boots had done. Several times a week she would read over all that she had written.

"It's one of the hardest mysteries I've ever tried to solve," she said to Joe. "I just stay confused."

"Well, it's the kind of mystery that doesn't hurt anything," Joe said. He was working on his rocket. He'd bought several models and was putting them together.

"I know. Somebody obviously loves Boots. I'd just like to know who it is."

The next afternoon the whole family went out into the yard for a rocket demonstration.

Joe sounded very important as he said, "Now you all stay back. This is the detonator, you see?" He had a small box in his hand. A wire went from the box to a foot-long rocket perched on a yellow launching pad.

Joe made them stand off to one side, then said, "All right. It's time for the countdown." He began counting, "Five—four—three—two—one!" He pushed a button, and suddenly the rocket began hissing. It took off, and all the Joneses craned their necks, watching it zoom toward the sky.

"Look at that thing go!" Joe said. "Am I a rocket man or not?"

When the rocket reached its utmost height, it suddenly popped open.

"And there's the parachute!" Juliet yelled. "It's floating down."

Everybody had to congratulate Joe.

"You will, no doubt, be a rocket scientist one day, Joe," Mr. Jones said.

Juliet said, "Can we do it again?"

"Sure. I've got six engines. We can do it six times."

It was later in the afternoon, when Juliet and Joe were in the house, that she said, "I'm glad Mom and Dad like to do things with us."

"Me too." Then he saw that Boots was scratching at Juliet's shoe. "What does he want?"

"Oh, he wants to go out. He's ready to start roaming again."

She picked up the cat and cuddled him. That seemed to satisfy Boots for a time. He began purring.

"Did you ever find that bootie that he lost?" Joe asked.

Last week Boots had disappeared while wearing his booties. When he came back, one was missing.

"No. I looked everywhere, but I couldn't find it."

"Well, he scratched it off somewhere. I wonder if whoever made them will make him a new one."

"They haven't yet. And I'm just dying of curiosity to know who is taking care of this cat."

Later that day, Juliet went for a walk and took Boots with her. This time she carried him, rather than let him down. She stopped at the house three yards down the street, where Mrs. Linton was out watering her flowers.

"You walking your cat, Juliet?" she called.

"No. He's not walking. I have to carry him."

"Why don't you put him down and let him walk?"

"Because he runs away."

"Runs away?"

"Yes, all the time!"

"I know that must worry you."

"I worry about him a lot."

Mrs. Linton put down the hose and walked over to the sidewalk. She petted Boots's smooth fur and said, "He sure is a pretty cat."

"The prettiest cat in the whole world."

Mrs. Linton smiled. "I'm sure there's a lot of little girls who are saying that about their cats. But he really is a beauty."

"I wish he'd stay home, but he won't. He just wanders around."

"We've all had pets that wander off. I had a cocker spaniel. We found him once clear on the other side of town."

"I've heard stories about how cats can find their way home. They have an instinct—like birds when they go on migrations."

"That's true. I read about a cat that walked all the way from California to Oklahoma to get back home. Got shut up in a truck and was carried off. It took him months, but he finally showed up—half starved and with sore feet."

"Oh, what a story! I hope that doesn't happen to Boots."

"Maybe you just need to keep him in the house all the time."

"I hate to do that. He likes the outside so much. Well, I've got to be going, Mrs. Linton."

"Good-bye, Juliet."

When Juliet went home, she said, "Mom, what would you think if I kept Boots in the house all the time?"

"I think he would drive us all crazy." But Mrs. Jones smiled. "You're just going to have to learn to live with that cat and his problem, Juliet."

"I suppose so. Well, let's go up and do our homework, Boots. We've got a lot to do—at least, I have."

OAK WOOD

The Clue

Juliet kept Boots in the house for three days. She hoped that he would finally calm down and learn to live inside. "He needs to be an inside cat," she told her mother.

But this had not worked. "That cat's driving me crazy, Juliet," her mother said. "You've got to let him out."

"But, Mom, I'm afraid something will happen to him!"

Juliet often took Boots along when she went to the nursing home. Going there had become a habit with some of the other boys and girls too. They had found out that visiting the old people was one of the most satisfying things that they could do. No matter when they went, or how many went, or how little time they had to spend, the patients were always glad to see them.

As Juliet and Joe walked in one day, they were greeted by one after another. Some were in wheelchairs. Some walked with a cane. Some were healthier than others. She knew most of their names by this time. It gave her a good feeling to know that she was doing something to make somebody happy. *Thank you, Lord, for this chance to help these people,* she prayed silently. *Make me always want to help people.*

Most of the boys and girls had adopted certain nursing home people as their special friends. They would divide up and go at once to those that they knew best, and Juliet always went to see Mrs. Eliza Jones. So today she went one way, and Joe went another.

When she walked into Mrs. Jones's room, Juliet found her talking with a nurse. But the old lady said right away, "Juliet, I'm so glad to see you!"

"I'm glad to see you, too, Mrs. Jones."

Mrs. Jones looked at her closely. She adjusted her glasses. She looked again. Then, in a disappointed voice she said, "You didn't bring Boots with you today."

"Not this time. We didn't come from home."

"Oh." She looked up at the nurse and said, "Juliet has the most wonderful cat you have ever seen."

"I know. I've been here a few times when she's brought him in," the nurse said. "It's nice of you to bring your kitten, Juliet. I hope you'll bring him back. All the patients like to see animals."

"Oh, I will," Juliet said quickly.

The nurse patted Mrs. Jones on the shoulder as she left. "You two have a nice visit."

Juliet said, "I brought you some fruit."

"Oranges! Oh, I love fruit. Why don't you help me peel an orange? My fingers aren't as strong as they once were."

So she peeled the orange and broke it into its small, wedge-shaped sections. When Mrs. Jones insisted, Juliet ate some of them, too.

"How are Lexy and Ben?" Juliet asked.

"Oh, they're fine," Mrs. Jones said. "They'll be coming to visit again this weekend."

Juliet was very pleased. "I do like them so much. I wish they lived here in town."

"Well, they may be moving here," Mrs. Jones said. "My daughter-in-law is trying to get my son to move. If he can get transferred, they will."

"That would be wonderful! Then we could do all kinds of things together."

They talked for a while, and then Mrs. Jones again said a little sadly, "I'm so sorry that you didn't bring Boots."

Juliet felt bad about this. She decided that Mrs. Jones was not having a very happy day. "I'll bring him the next time I come. I promise."

"I hope you will."

“The trouble is that he runs away so much,” Juliet said. “We just can’t keep up with him, and I’m afraid something bad will happen to him.”

“Oh, that would be awful!” Mrs. Jones replied.

They talked some more about Ben and Lexy, and then Juliet got up. “I’ve got to visit some other folks now. But I’ll be sure to bring Boots next time I come.”

“Do. I love that precious kitten.”

Juliet visited several other patients. She had discovered that there were many lonely people in the nursing home. She had also discovered that some had wonderful stories to tell about the old days. She loved to hear them talk. One lady told her about making homemade soap, and Juliet was fascinated.

“And it was better than any soap you can find today,” the lady said. She was in her nineties, but her mind was sharp and clear.

“I wish I knew how to make soap.”

“Well, I wish I was back home and you could visit me. I’d show you how. I made it out in the backyard in a big iron pot.”

It was a sunshiny day and still the middle of the afternoon. So on the way home, Juliet and Joe stopped off to play awhile in the park. A wild pecan tree grew there, and they found some nuts on the ground left over from last fall. "They probably won't taste very good," Juliet said, "but we'll see."

On the other side of the park, they found Chili and Flash shooting baskets. Every moment the two boys were not studying or working, they seemed to be playing basketball.

Joe joined them, but Juliet just watched for a while. She was not good at shooting baskets. Flash was the best. Even from his chair, he could put the ball through the hoop much of the time.

"Just wait until I get on my feet," he said. "After God heals me, I'm going to be a great ball player."

"You're great now," Chili said. His face gleamed. "You're better than I am, and I'm the best."

Flash grinned. "That makes me better than the best."

Tired of watching, Juliet wandered off on her own. She sat on the grass beside some heavy bushes. A bird overhead was singing a beautiful song. She couldn't tell what kind it was, but she watched it and enjoyed its singing. A gray squirrel came down a tree, looked at her, and chattered angrily.

"Are you mad at me for visiting?" Juliet asked him.

The squirrel watched her with his bright eyes. He chattered again, as though talking to her, and then scampered behind the tree.

With a laugh, Juliet started to get up to chase him. Just as she did, something in the grass caught her eye. It was something blue. She stooped and looked more closely. She gasped and picked it up.

"It's the bootie that Boots lost!" she said. "Now we know he comes this way when he leaves home. Maybe this mystery will get solved after all. And soon, I hope."

She ran back to get Joe. "Joe! Come here! I found the bootie that Boots lost."

"Where?" He bounced the basketball to Chili and ran toward her.

Flash and Chili followed him, and Juliet had to explain to the other boys what had happened.

"You mean that cat of yours wears shoes?" Chili asked with amazement. "I never heard of no cat wearing shoes."

"They're not shoes. They're little booties—like this. See? It's what babies wear, but this one was made extra small—especially for Boots."

"So who made it?" Chili asked.

"I don't know who made it. That's the problem. It's a mystery. He goes off and comes back wearing handkerchiefs around his neck, and booties, and ribbons, and flower necklaces. And whoever does it feeds him, too. He'll hardly eat anything at home."

"Well, if you found one bootie, the rest must be someplace."

"No, no, that's all he lost. Just one. But let's go take a look around."

Flash led the way. He could travel faster in his wheelchair than the rest of them could run. When they got to the place where she had found the bootie, they decided to spread out and look for clues.

Juliet just walked around. She didn't even know what she was looking for. After a while she heard somebody calling. She followed the sound of the voice and found Chili and Flash and Joe all looking at the ground.

"Look at this," Chili said.

Juliet went closer and saw paw prints in the soft earth at the edge of a flowerbed.

"Reckon that's your cat?" Flash asked.

"Oh, I don't know, Flash. There are lots of cats around here."

"Better not get too excited," Joe agreed. "There are more cats in the world than just Boots."

Juliet, however, said, "It may not be him, but it might be. Let's follow the tracks. It looks like they keep going for a while. Don't step on them. We may want to come back and look at them later."

They followed the paw prints to where they stopped—right where the strip of soft dirt stopped.

Juliet saw that they were close to where the nursing home lawn went one way and the woods went the other. She said, "Which way would he have gone from here? There's no way to figure it out."

For a while they argued over where the cat might have gone, then finally gave up and walked back to the play area. The boys returned to shooting baskets.

"See you later—at home," Joe said.

Juliet saw Jenny at the swings. They swung and talked—about school lessons, about a new pizza place in town, about their trip to the TV station, and about Boots. Juliet said, "Somehow I just think those pawprints belong to Boots."

"Maybe we could get him and bring him here and see if they fit. You know—just put his foot down in one paw print."

"Yes, we could do that," Juliet agreed.

Later, as they made their way home, Juliet said, "I've been thinking of a plan to track Boots down once and for all."

"What is it?" Jenny asked.

"No. I have to get it all straight in my mind first, but I'll tell you tomorrow morning."

They reached Jenny's house and found Delores waiting.

Juliet said, "Delores, I'm going to set a trap to find out where my cat goes. I think I'll need you and Jenny to help me."

"Sure. Then we'll *all* be detectives."

The girls agreed to help the next morning,

and Juliet slowly walked on toward home. By the time she reached the Jones house, she had finished putting her plan together.

Then Too Smart Jones took a deep breath and said to herself, *This cat mystery has gone on long enough. I'm going to solve this case tomorrow, or I'll know the reason why!*

200

The Cat's Secret

After breakfast the next morning, Juliet picked up a pencil and opened the notebook she had named *The Adventures of Boots.* She wrote, "This is the day I'm going to solve this case. The mystery of the wandering cat."

Boots was already clawing at her bedroom door, wanting out again.

Juliet said, "You just wait. This time we're going to find out where you go when you hide from me."

Boots scratched at the door again, saying, "*Mrow!*" in a most pitiful voice. It was almost as if he said, "Please let me out. I can't stand it in here any longer."

Next, Juliet went to her dresser and took out a ribbon that had a small bell attached. "You come here," she said. "We're going to bell the cat this time."

Boots did not protest when Juliet tied the bell around his neck. He did paw at it when it tinkled. However, he was soon again ready to be let out.

First, Juliet phoned Jenny. "Is that you, Jenny?"

"Yes. Is this Juliet?"

"Yes, and we're about ready to spring our trap. Will you be in position?"

"Yes. I'm leaving right now."

"Be at those bushes in the park where I found the bootie. All right?"

"I'll be there."

She hung up the phone and dialed another number.

"Delores?"

"Yes."

"It's me. Are you ready?"

"I'm ready," Delores said. "I'll be where you told me to be."

"All right, then. We're going to catch him this time." Juliet picked up Boots. "Here we go," she said. She went downstairs.

In the kitchen, her mother looked at her. "What's that you've got around Boots's neck?"

"It's a bell." She tinkled it with her finger. "See how clear it sounds."

"So you belled the cat. You're going to follow him by sound."

"More than that. I've got the girls all staked

out. We're going to follow this cat and find out where he goes, once and for all."

"That sounds like a good idea. I hope it works."

"It will. It's just got to work."

Juliet opened the back door and stepped outside. She put Boots down. "Now, I know you're going to run off, so get at it."

Sure enough, Boots took off for the hedge and disappeared. Juliet had on her hiking shoes and a pair of jeans so that she wouldn't scratch her legs. She sped around the hedge, but of course the cat was already gone. She ran hard until she came to the park.

There Jenny was waiting in her appointed place and waving her hands. "He just went by here!" she yelled excitedly. "He went that way!"

"Come with me!" Juliet cried. "We've got to keep up with him!"

The girls ran as fast as they could, and soon they reached the spot where Delores was waiting. "Have you seen Boots?"

"Yes. He came by here. I heard the bell tinkling, and then I saw him. He went that way—over toward the nursing home."

"Let's go!"

Juliet and her two friends ran hard again. They reached the nursing home. Juliet looked around, disappointed. She did not see Boots anywhere.

"He's got to be around here somewhere,"

Delores insisted. “He came right over this way. I saw him.”

“There are a lot of bushes around the nursing home. Maybe he’s under one of them. Let’s walk all the way around,” Juliet said.

They started around the side of the nursing home.

Suddenly Juliet cried, “There he is!”

“Where?”

“Over there by the building! See? Look, he’s climbing that tree beside the window!”

The little bell tinkled as Boots scrambled up. Then he ran out on a limb and jumped onto a window ledge.

“Let’s get him down from there!” Delores cried.

“No, let’s wait and see what happens. Now we know he comes here, but we don’t know who he comes to see.”

At that moment the window opened, and two hands reached out. The hands picked up Boots and took him inside.

“That’s it!” Juliet exclaimed. “Now let’s see who lives there.”

The girls broke into a run and raced to the window. But when they came to a stop, panting, they could not see inside. The blind was closed.

Delores said, “We could go inside, but we wouldn’t know which room this is.”

“I know what we could do,” Juliet said.

"We'll count the number of windows over to the right and then the number to the left. Then we'll go inside and count the doors. And then we'll know which room is this one."

Jenny grinned. "That sounds like Too Smart Jones."

They counted.

"There are seven windows to the right and there are six windows to the left," Juliet said. "We ought to be able to find it."

They jogged around to the front entrance, where a nurse met them.

"We need to see whoever is in the room that's seven windows from that way and six windows from this way," Juliet said.

"What did you say?"

"Oh, that's all right. We'll find it."

The girls began to walk down the hall. The problem was that not all the doors were to a patient's room. Some of them went to private offices. Maybe they had more than one window. Some went to storage rooms. It was confusing.

They walked on. Finally Delores, discouraged, said, "I don't think this is going to work."

But at that moment Juliet heard something.

"Did you hear that?" she cried.

"I did!" Jenny said. "It's a little bell!"

"It's the bell on Boots's collar. Let's find it."

They moved down the hall slowly, listening. Sometimes the tinkling sound stopped for a while and then would start again. But the tinkling kept getting louder.

Juliet was just starting to think that this hall seemed very familiar, when suddenly she heard a clear *"Mrow!"*

"That's it!" She looked above the door and saw the room number. "Number one fifteen! Why, that's Mrs. Jones's room."

Juliet knocked, and at once a happy voice said, "Come in."

Juliet opened the door. Then she stopped so fast that her two friends ran into her from behind. "Mrs. Jones," she said, "you've got Boots!"

There Boots sat—in Mrs. Eliza Jones's lap.

The old lady looked guilty. "I'm afraid I have. He comes to visit me all the time. I guess I should have told you about it, but—"

"Oh, it's all right, Mrs. Jones," Juliet said. "I'm just relieved to find he's with you. We didn't know where in the world he went."

"I've got all the things to take care of him when he comes. See?"

Juliet saw a water bowl. She saw a food dish on the floor and several things that were obviously cat toys.

Mrs. Jones was stroking Boots with a brush. She said quietly with a smile, "He just comes and goes. I'm always so glad to see him.

He's brought a lot of sunshine into my life, Juliet. I can't tell you how much."

"Well, he couldn't be with anyone that would love him any better," Juliet said.

Jenny and Delores both began to laugh. "The answer to the mystery was here all the time!"

Juliet nodded happily. "That's right."

"The first time I saw him without you, I was in my wheelchair out in the lobby. He was in the yard, and I had the nurse bring him in. When he wanted to leave, I just opened the window and let him out." She smiled. "He was back at my window the next day. I think he goes up and down the tree."

"He likes trees. And I guess he was looking for tender loving care. We all need TLC, don't we?"

"I know I should have told you about him coming. And I'm sorry I didn't. I guess I was afraid you wouldn't want him to come on his own."

"It's all right now that I know where he is. We'll share him. He'll be your cat and my cat."

"Oh, Juliet, that's the sweetest thing! It's made me so happy."

When it was time for the girls to go home, Juliet said, "I'll just leave Boots with you for now. I'm sure he'll find his way home."

"God bless you, dear girl," Mrs. Jones said. "He brings me so much happiness. So do you."

As soon as they left, Juliet looked up at the sky and took a deep breath. "Thank You, Lord. You do such nice things for people." Then she turned to her friends and grinned broadly. "And that's that," she said. "Another mystery solved!"

"Too Smart Jones, girl detective, solves another case," Jenny said. She hugged her friend, and Delores hugged both of them. And then the three girls headed for the ice cream parlor.

Get swept away in the many Gilbert Morris Adventures available from Moody Press:

"Too Smart" Jones

4025-8 Pool Party Thief
4026-6 Buried Jewels
4027-4 Disappearing Dogs
4028-2 Dangerous Woman
4029-0 Stranger in the Cave
4030-4 Cat's Secret
4031-2 Stolen Bicycle
4032-0 Wilderness Mystery

Come along for the adventures and mysteries Juliet "Too Smart" Jones always manages to find. She and her other homeschool friends solve these great adventures and learn biblical truths along the way.
Ages 9-14

Seven Sleepers - The Lost Chronicles

3667-6 The Spell of the Crystal Chair
3668-4 The Savage Game of Lord Zarak
3669-2 The Strange Creatures of Dr. Korbo
3670-6 City of the Cyborgs

More exciting adventures from the Seven Sleepers. As these exciting young people attempt to faithfully follow Goél, they learn important moral and spiritual lessons. Come along with them as they encounter danger, intrigue, and mystery.
Ages 10-14

Dixie Morris Animal Adventures

3363-4 Dixie and Jumbo
3364-2 Dixie and Stripes
3365-0 Dixie and Dolly
3366-9 Dixie and Sandy
3367-7 Dixie and Ivan
3368-5 Dixie and Bandit
3369-3 Dixie and Champ
3370-7 Dixie and Perry
3371-5 Dixie and Blizzard
3382-3 Dixie and Flash

Follow the exciting adventures of this animal lover as she learns more of God and His character through her many adventures underneath the Big Top. Ages 9-14

The Daystar Voyages

4102-X Secret of the Planet Makon
4106-8 Wizards of the Galaxy
4107-6 Escape From the Red Comet
4108-4 Dark Spell Over Morlandria
4109-2 Revenge of the Space Pirates
4110-6 Invasion of the Killer Locusts
4111-4 Dangers of the Rainbow Nebula
4112-2 The Frozen Space Pilot

Join the crew of the Daystar as they traverse the wide expanse of space. Adventure and danger abound, but they learn time and again that God is truly the Master of the Universe. Ages 10-14

Seven Sleepers Series

3681-1 Flight of the Eagles
3682-X The Gates of Neptune
3683-3 The Swords of Camelot
3684-6 The Caves That Time Forgot
3685-4 Winged Riders of the Desert
3686-2 Empress of the Underworld
3687-0 Voyage of the Dolphin
3691-9 Attack of the Amazons
3692-7 Escape with the Dream Maker
3693-5 The Final Kingdom

Go with Josh and his friends as they are sent by Goél, their spiritual leader, on dangerous and challenging voyages to conquer the forces of darkness in the new world. Ages 10-14

Bonnets and Bugles Series

0911-3 Drummer Boy at Bull Run
0912-1 Yankee Belles in Dixie
0913-X The Secret of Richmond Manor
0914-8 The Soldier Boy's Discovery
0915-6 Blockade Runner
0916-4 The Gallant Boys of Gettysburg
0917-2 The Battle of Lookout Mountain
0918-0 Encounter at Cold Harbor
0919-9 Fire Over Atlanta
0920-2 Bring the Boys Home

Follow good friends Leah Carter and Jeff Majors as they experience danger, intrigue, compassion, and love in these civil war adventures. Ages 10-14

Moody Press, a ministry of the
Moody Bible Institute, is designed for education,
evangelization, and edification. If we may assist you
in knowing more about Christ and the Christian
life, please write us without obligation:
Moody Press, c/o MLM, Chicago, IL 60610.